HIDDEN HEARTACHE

Doctor Emma Bradshaw's life is disrupted when Nick Rudd arrives back in town to take up a post at the GP practice where she works. It's not so easy to ignore the love of your life when you have to see him every day, but Emma is keeping her distance — Nick let her down badly in the past. Now, though, he'll do anything to rekindle the trust and love she once showed him . . .

Books by Suzanna Ross
in the Linford Romance Library:

TRUST IN ME

SPECIAL MESSAGE TO READERS

THE ULVERSCROFT FOUNDATION
(registered UK charity number 264873)
was established in 1972 to provide funds for research, diagnosis and treatment of eye diseases. Examples of major projects funded by the Ulverscroft Foundation are:-

- The Children's Eye Unit at Moorfields Eye Hospital, London
- The Ulverscroft Children's Eye Unit at Great Ormond Street Hospital for Sick Children
- Funding research into eye diseases and treatment at the Department of Ophthalmology, University of Leicester
- The Ulverscroft Vision Research Group, Institute of Child Health
- Twin operating theatres at the Western Ophthalmic Hospital, London
- The Chair of Ophthalmology at the Royal Australian College of Ophthalmologists

You can help further the work of the Foundation by making a donation or leaving a legacy. Every contribution is gratefully received. If you would like to help support the Foundation or require further information, please contact:

THE ULVERSCROFT FOUNDATION
The Green, Bradgate Road, Anstey
Leicester LE7 7FU, England
Tel: (0116) 236 4325

website: www.foundation.ulverscroft.com

SUZANNA ROSS

HIDDEN HEARTACHE

Complete and Unabridged

LINFORD
Leicester

First published in Great Britain in 2013

First Linford Edition
published 2014

*A catalogue record for this book is available
from the British Library.*

ISBN 978–1–4448–1830–7

Published by
F. A. Thorpe (Publishing)
Anstey, Leicestershire

Set by Words & Graphics Ltd.
Anstey, Leicestershire
Printed and bound in Great Britain by
T. J. International Ltd., Padstow, Cornwall

This book is printed on acid-free paper

1

The Harley-Davidson came to a stop within feet of where Dr Emma Bradshaw was stowing her bag in the boot of her yellow VW Beetle. Startled, she glanced up, squinting into the late afternoon sunshine as she tried to see who was there. The breath caught in her throat as she watched the rider dismount and take two long strides until he was standing inches away.

His leathers were sinfully tight — moulding his body with the faithful touch of a lover. He had a great body, Emma acknowledged grudgingly. And he was tall — at least six foot four — she had to crick her neck to look up at him.

With restless fingers, she pulled at the silver-grey jacket of her suit, smoothing it down over the waistband of her skirt. She was respectably dressed and yet she'd never felt so exposed and vulnerable.

She waved in the general direction of the building, unable to take her eyes off him.

'I'm afraid the surgery's closed this afternoon.' Her voice was annoyingly high-pitched and she coughed in an attempt to clear her throat. 'Is it an emergency?'

His visor was still down and she wished he'd remove his biker's helmet. It might add to the mystery, but it was also very disconcerting.

As though he'd read her mind, he reached up and removed the offending headgear.

Oh, yes. She very nearly fanned herself on the spot. The face definitely lived up to everything his body had promised. His blond hair might be a bit long, but he was utterly gorgeous.

'No emergency.' His voice was low and playful and sent unwelcome shivers down her spine.

Edible — the word sprang to her

mind unbidden. Shocked, she realised she shouldn't be looking at a patient like this. Tearing her eyes from him, she turned and slammed down the boot lid.

'In that case, perhaps you'd like to call back tomorrow morning. We open at eight-thirty.'

He gave a lazy grin and she felt something flutter in her tummy. 'This can't wait until morning.'

Her eyes narrowed as they swept back to his face. There was something about him . . . Had she treated him before? No, definitely not — if he was on her list she'd have remembered. Thick lashes fringed laughing blue eyes — laughing at her, she just knew it.

Immediately, she was on her guard. She should be used to being laughed at, but she wasn't and it hurt that this gorgeous stranger saw fit to ridicule her now.

'Spit it out, then,' she told him sharply. 'I don't have time to stand in the car park playing games. I have patients to see.'

'Then have dinner with me later, after you've done all your home visits.'

She shook her head. This was becoming surreal. Strange men didn't drop by to ask Emma out on dates — particularly not strange men who were off the scale on the hotness barometer. But that easy manner and those blue eyes did look familiar . . . She frowned, trying and failing to place him.

'Have we met?'

He took another step towards her and her gaze fixed on his mouth. She watched his lips curve again and a scar on his upper lip caught her attention. It was faded, barely there; if he hadn't been standing so close she'd never have seen it. It was the type of scar that might have resulted from a childhood accident such as falling face first onto the corner of a table . . .

She drew a ragged breath as a wave of nausea hit her. She hadn't seen that scar for fourteen years. She staggered back, came hard up against the side of her car and was grateful for the support it offered.

'*Nick?*' she queried disbelievingly.

'It's been a long time, Emma. How have you been?'

The boy who'd haunted her dreams and her nightmares for as long as she could remember. How had she not recognised him?

In her defence, she hadn't been expecting to see him again, not after all these years. And he'd changed — he'd grown from a heartbreakingly beautiful boy of sixteen into a man of such raw sex appeal that just looking at him took her breath away. She should have known it was him, from her reaction the moment she'd seen him ride into the health centre car park on that bike. No other man had ever made her heart beat faster or elicited wicked thoughts with just a look — none had even come close. Of course — it *had* to be Nick.

The pain took her unawares — a searing ache in her chest. For a minute she thought she was having a heart attack, but quickly realised it was simply a physical manifestation of fourteen years of mental torment.

'What are you doing back?'

He shrugged a broad shoulder. 'I've a lot of history here.'

'Sometimes history's best left in the past.'

He ignored the jibe. 'Tell me, did you miss me?'

The question was so ludicrous, she didn't know how she managed not to laugh in his face. She'd missed him more than she'd ever thought possible — and yet, at the same time, she'd hoped never to lay eyes on him again as long as she lived. From somewhere, she mustered the dirtiest look from her dirty looks repertoire and hoped he'd take the hint and go.

She wished she hadn't bothered when he took another step closer. One more and she'd be able to touch him . . .

'Because I missed you, Em.'

She took a deep breath. 'I don't need

to listen to this nonsense.' She pushed herself away from the reassuring support of her car. 'I've a lot to do before I can finish up for the night.'

'Em, wait.' His hand was outstretched, but she dodged out of his reach.

'Don't touch me.'

'You used to like it when I touched you.'

She gave a humourless laugh. 'That was a long time ago — I was young and foolish.'

'You were never foolish, Emma.'

She shook her head. He didn't know the half of it. The entire town thought her very foolish indeed. Even now, as a respected doctor, her youthful folly hadn't been forgotten in some quarters. But none of that mattered now. What mattered was survival — and getting out of here while she still could.

'Nick — I . . . It was nice to see you again.' An outright lie — but she needed to cling to her veneer of politeness. 'If you ever visit town again — '

She was going to tell him not to

bother looking her up, but the words died on her lips. Before he could delay her any further, she jumped into her car and drove off.

There was so much she should have told him — but he'd be gone soon enough, and then she probably never would see him again. What was the point in picking over old wounds?

Besides, Mrs Smith was waiting for her visit.

* * *

Nick frowned as he watched her drive away. He'd hardly expected a hero's welcome, not after all those years. But, at one time, Emma had been the only one in Tullibaird who'd believed in him and he'd expected she might show some sign of being pleased he'd returned. Instead, Dr Bradshaw had made it abundantly clear she was horrified by his reappearance in her life. She hadn't been able to wait to get away.

He jammed his helmet back on and the bike roared into life.

Physically, she'd barely changed since he'd left. The jeans and T-shirts she'd favoured when he'd last known her had been replaced by a smart suit, and the pale blonde hair she'd always worn loose about her shoulders was pinned back now. But the fine bone structure, the dainty physique, were the same. And despite the weariness he'd detected, she didn't look a day older.

The fun had left her, though. Where he remembered a happy, laughing girl, she was now a woman who seemed to have the troubles of the world weighing down her soul. Something had happened, and he fully intended to find out what. Nick was back for answers and he wasn't leaving until he got them.

* * *

'Are you okay, Emma?' Annie, the practice nurse asked as they trooped into one of the consulting rooms for the scheduled practice meeting next morning.

'Just a bit tired.' She smiled. She'd slept very badly — not surprising, really. The nightmares had never left her completely, but last night, after seeing Nick, she'd dreamed in glorious detail once again and it hadn't been pretty.

'The new doctor should be here soon. Hopefully he'll take some of the strain from you and Angus.'

Sandy — a doctor in the practice — had suffered a recent heart attack and had been forced into early retirement. That had left Emma and the senior partner, Angus McDonald, under some pressure. Of course the services of a locum had been secured, but that wasn't the same. The townsfolk were set in their ways — they preferred to consult a doctor they knew.

'I've asked Dr Rudd to join us this morning,' Angus informed them as soon as they'd all gathered. 'He's not officially starting work until next week, but he moved back to town yesterday and I thought it would be useful for everyone to meet him as soon as possible.'

Moved back yesterday? That was odd — the same time as Nick had turned up. Emma shook her head. Thankfully, that wasn't a possibility — Nick was frighteningly intelligent, no doubt about that, but he hadn't been interested in academic work when she'd known him. There no way he could have gained the necessary grades to study medicine. Besides, Nick's surname was Malone.

'We're very lucky to have him,' Angus continued. 'He spent some time locally when he was a child, so people will know him.' He glanced across at Emma. 'It seems Tullibaird is particularly good at growing its own medical talent.'

Emma smiled obligingly while trying to remember whether she knew a local family named Rudd. Of course, in all likelihood they would have been away before her time. She was only grateful that Angus had found someone to take up the post, and so quickly. They'd been concerned that it might be a struggle — Tullibaird was a tiny town, remote by any standards. People were often reluctant to move here.

The door opened and Emma glanced up to see Claire, the practice manager, enter to join the meeting, followed by . . .

'Nick.' Emma's mouth was suddenly dry. How much bad luck could one girl have? She must have been a pit bull terrier in a previous life, and this was payback — it was the only explanation. 'Please tell me you're not the new doctor.'

He looked devastating today — even more so than yesterday. The biker leathers were gone. He was in a charcoal grey suit with a shirt so white he must have used a certain brand of well-known washing powder. His tanned face broke into a grin, his blue eyes crinkling irresistibly, and she could sense Annie and Claire's increased interest.

'Anything to oblige a lady. I'm not the new doctor.' He grinned.

'Really?'

Angus laughed and rose to his feet to beckon Nick further into the room. 'Of course he's the new doctor. Nick, come in and meet everyone.'

* * *

'Dr Rudd?' she asked pointedly when they were alone in her consulting room later. He'd followed her in on the pretext of wanting to discuss the workings of the local community, and she'd been powerless to stop him without causing a scene. And Emma didn't like scenes. 'What happened to Malone?'

'I changed it. Malone had too many bad memories.'

She nodded briefly. That couldn't be argued with. 'You could have warned me about this yesterday.'

'I would have, if you hadn't bolted.'

He sat on the corner of her desk, looming over her — taking on the body language of superiority. Well, she wasn't impressed . . . not even slightly.

'It was really mean,' she persisted. 'Letting me find out in the meeting in front of everyone.'

'Emma.' There was laughter in his voice. 'Since when have either of us cared what others think of us?'

'I might not have cared once, but I do now.'

He was thoughtful for a moment. 'Ah. Well, I guess that explains a lot.'

'And you *should* care, too. If you're going to treat people in this community you need to earn their respect.'

She watched as his hard jaw clenched. She'd hit a nerve. It was unintentional, but she was glad to see this chink in his hard-man armour. When she'd seen him yesterday, he'd given off an aura of invincibility that, quite frankly, had her running scared. Nick had always been warm and passionate — with her, at least. She was pleased to see he wasn't completely devoid of emotion these days, after all.

He shifted closer and crossed his arms. 'I didn't come in here for an argument.'

'Then you're going to be disappointed, because an argument's all that's on offer.'

'We're going to be working together. Don't you think we should find some way to get along?' He sounded so reasonable, damn him. And he was right — she hated that. It would be unforgivably unprofessional if they were continuously at each other's throats.

'What happened between us was a long time ago. Don't you think we can put it behind us? Pretend we just met?'

His suggestion couldn't have shown more clearly how differently they viewed their teenage romance. There was no way she could forget, ever.

Their relationship had meant the world to her — and cost her everything. And now he was suggesting it all be consigned to the archives, forgotten as if it had meant nothing! She hadn't realised until then that, on some level, she'd always hoped he'd suffered from their separation, too.

'I — ' she squawked, appalled. 'I can't actually believe you just said that.'

He got off the desk and sat back on his heels in front of her. It was only when he brushed her cheek with the back of his fingers that she realised she was crying. She wanted to recoil from his touch, but her body remembered him and sprang to life totally against her will. She gasped as a yearning she hadn't felt in fourteen years began as a coiling need deep in her abdomen — and she felt its effect all the way down to her toes.

'I'm not worth your tears, Emma,' he told her softly.

That was her undoing — the physical pull she could have ignored, but the soft tone he'd always used when he spoke to her was irresistible. She wasn't even aware she'd leaned in towards him until she felt their lips touch and, without warning, she was transported back . . .

* * *

Her lips were soft and sweet and everything he remembered. Now he was sure he'd done the right thing in coming back. Nick drew her gently to her feet and deepened the kiss — and she let him. She still wanted him; he could tell from the way her lips moved beneath his, the way her fingers clung to the soft cotton of his shirt. When she slipped her hand beneath the material, he drew a sharp breath of air into his lungs. Her hand on his bare skin felt so right — but knew he had to put a stop to it, or they'd end up making love on her desk.

'Emma.' He drew away. 'We can't — not here.'

Her eyes snapped open and quickly she put as much distance as she could between them.

'We can't anywhere. That was a

one-off. I don't want to kiss you again.'

'I know you're angry about the way I left, but what we had was good. And I think we could still have something, if we gave it a chance.'

She looked at him as though he'd just crawled out of a swamp.

'I'm sorry if I gave you the wrong impression just now, but I'm really not looking to revisit any teen fantasies . . . and, at your age, neither should you be.'

Well, that put him in his place. But he knew she wanted him — he could see it in her eyes — and he was determined to wait as long as it took for her to realise it too. He might not have been equipped to fight for her when he was sixteen, but he'd spent the last fourteen years making sure he was prepared — and this time he wouldn't be giving up.

2

Emma sniffed as the aroma of home cooking met her in the hallway — shepherd's pie, if she wasn't mistaken.

Her mother had obviously let herself in, again. She knew Moira only fussed out of concern, but it was high time she realised Emma could take care of herself. Maybe it was even time Emma asked for her key back.

She let the door shut with a slam.

'I'm in the kitchen,' Moira called. 'Have you heard the news? *He's* back.'

Emma closed her eyes and leaned back against the wall. It had obviously been too much to hope that the news wouldn't have reached Moira yet. Emma should have known better. Moira was well known for being able to ferret out any gossip within a hundred-mile radius.

'Who's back?' she called wearily,

playing for time, ill-equipped to deal with what she knew was coming next. Even if she lived to be a hundred, she wouldn't be ready.

'That boy.'

Emma opened her eyes to find Moira had advanced into the hallway. She must be desperate to discuss the new turn of events because, normally, it was well-nigh impossible to prise her out of the kitchen when there was a meal to be prepared.

'His name's Nick, Mum. You can say his name — it won't kill you.'

'Well?'

'Yes, I know Nick's back.'

She watched as Moira's lips pursed. 'Have you seen him?'

Emma urged herself to be calm. She was no longer a frightened sixteen-year-old, she was a grown woman with a responsible job. And she was certainly capable of choosing whom she could see. 'Yes.'

Moira's disapproval was an almost tangible force. It reached down Emma's throat and almost made her throw up on the spot. She couldn't handle her mother's dislike of Nick — had never been able to handle it. Even when she wanted so much to hate him herself, she still bristled at Moira's negative reaction.

'He's no good, you know.'

'Mum . . . '

'Everything that happened was his fault. Don't you remember what you went through, Emma? He tore your heart into pieces. He left you so broken that you haven't been able to face another relationship. You sit in on your own, night after night, with only your books for company. If I didn't pop by to feed you I'm sure you'd forget to eat most of the time. And *he* did that to you.'

Emma said nothing. If she spoke, she knew there'd be an argument. It was pathetic that she still felt so protective of Nick, but she couldn't help it.

Avoidance — a tactic she was fond of using. She found changing the subject infinitely preferable to raking up the past.

'Is tea ready?' she asked with a hopeful air.

Moira stared at her for a long moment and then seemed to reach a decision. 'It'll be five minutes. Why don't you go and freshen up?'

Emma nodded, grateful for the chance to escape. She had one foot on the stairs, sure she'd got away with it, when her mother went for the jugular.

'Did you tell him?'

Emma froze mid-step and gasped. Tears stung the back of her eyes and she blinked them away furiously before giving a careless shrug. 'After all this time, what would be the point?'

'Oh, Emma.' Moira sighed and held out her arms. 'Come here.'

Emma allowed herself to be enveloped in her mother's arms. And it was only then that she began to sob.

Moira held her tight until she was able to pull herself together. Finally, she gave one last hiccup and pulled away, but winced as she registered the concern on her mother's face.

'I'm fine, honestly,' she protested — although she was sure it was blatantly obvious that she was anything but.

'I knew this would upset you. He's no business coming back after all this time.'

'Mum, please. I really don't want to talk about Nick. Or anything else.'

Moira sighed. 'Okay, if that's really how you feel. Go and rinse your face. I'll have dinner on the table by the time you come down.'

Emma was shocked by the pallor of her reflection in the bathroom mirror. Despite the reddened eyes and runny nose — evidence of her recent tears — she looked like a ghost.

Why did he have to come back now?

Quickly she rinsed her face with cold water and went into the bedroom to get changed. Jeans and a T-shirt were a relief after the formal attire she'd worn all day and Emma shook her hair loose before going back downstairs.

She felt more like herself now. She just needed to put Nick from her mind. But that was easier said than done, especially as the memory of his kiss was still warm on her lips.

'Feeling better?'

Emma nodded and sat down at the table. Her mother might be over-protective, but she was also a terrific cook and, surprisingly after the day she'd had, Emma was starving.

'Jan phoned just before you got in.'

'Oh?' Emma wondered what her best friend wanted. Her very pregnant best friend. 'Is she okay?'

'Seemed to be. She didn't leave a message. Said she'll call again later.'

It was a while since Emma had spoken to Jan and she missed having her best friend close by. Not long after she'd married, Jan had moved out of town. She now lived the rural life — and seemed to love it.

'How far along is she now?'

Emma bit the soft underside of her

lip. 'Thirty-five weeks.'

Moira nodded, but thankfully said no more. Neither did she hang around after they'd finished their meal, and Emma was glad. She loved her mum, really she did, but Moira had a tendency to try and run every aspect of Emma's life. She really needed to be on her own to sort out her feelings. She quickly cleared and washed the dishes, but couldn't settle to anything.

A walk. That was as good an idea as any. Fresh air might help and her mind always worked best when she was out in the open.

Emma shrugged on her jacket, picked up her mobile and keys, and closed the door behind her. A chill hung in the air as the promise of autumn made its presence known, but there were still a couple of hours of light left. Enough for her to make her way out of town, through the wood and up on to the hill.

She stopped briefly to admire the scenery. She may have been born in Tullibaird, but her surroundings never failed to stun her. She was lucky in so many ways, she reflected as she embarked on the steep incline that would take her to her favourite thinking place. Here she had room to breathe, and the freedom to roam.

In places the path was steep and the stones loose. Rather than dwelling on Nick's return, she used all her concentration to avoid tumbling down the sheer face of the ravine to the stream that bubbled at the bottom. Eventually, she cleared the trees and bracken and her pace slowed as she realised the spot she was making for was very much occupied.

Of course it would be — on some level she must have known, however much she tried to deny it to herself — this had been his favourite place, too. Half way up the hill, the shadow of the higher peaks offered protection, but the spot was elevated enough to afford a breathtaking view of the small town in its entirety. He sat now, as he always had, with one, long, denim-clad leg thrown carelessly up on the rock and leaning back on one hand. Strong, powerful and so utterly perfect to look at, her bones felt as though they were melting.

For a moment she considered turning and running, but she knew she'd have to face him sometime. Besides, something drew her closer — and she realised she didn't want to run anywhere. Not yet, at least.

'Nick.' She spoke his name softly, and watched as he turned. His smile took her breath away.

* * *

Her voice was barely more than a whisper, so quiet he thought he might have imagined it, as he had done many times over their years apart. But, when he turned, she was there, the evening sunshine catching in her hair and turning it to vibrant gold.

He had hoped she'd come. If he was honest, he hadn't really expected her to but he'd hoped nonetheless. This had been their spot — the place they'd come to when they wanted to be alone. They'd talked their youthful troubles away here. He hoped that, if they managed to reopen the lines of communication, they might be able to recapture the closeness they'd once shared.

'Hello, Emma.'

She stood motionless, staring at him with her baby-blue eyes and it was all he could do not to rush to her and gather her up in his arms. But he knew he couldn't rush her. He needed to win her trust, be her friend again, before he could hope for anything more.

She sat beside him on the rock, just beyond his reach. If he stretched out his arm just a fraction, the tips of his fingers would meet hers. The thought of touching her again, even in such an innocent way, made his heart race.

'You never said you wanted to be a doctor.' Her voice was clipped, businesslike, and she made the remark sound like an accusation.

He felt the corners of his mouth curve. She was on the offensive — feeling vulnerable and wanting to disguise the fact.

'Neither did you.'

They'd talked of plans for a future together, but both had still been at school. The world of work had been a promise that stretched out in front of them — something to aspire to. With so many possibilities, however, neither had narrowed their choices at that stage.

She sighed as though the world was weighing on her slender shoulders. And all he wanted to do was to bring a smile to her face. The Emma he remembered had never been without a smile — for him, at least. He couldn't believe his leaving could have affected her to this extent. Made her so wary. There had to be something more to the unhappiness he could see in her eyes.

'Why did you go into medicine?' he asked at last when she didn't speak.

'I spent some time in hospital after

you left. The medical staff were wonderful. I just wanted to give something back. Make a difference. You know?'

He nodded. Yes, he'd known the compelling urge to make a difference himself. That's what had driven him through the relentless years of study and training. It hadn't been easy for him; although he knew he was intelligent, he hadn't been the book-smart kind of clever that medical school demanded. He'd had to put the brakes on his youthful, carefree life and quickly turn himself around.

But it had been worth it. He glanced over at Emma and smiled. Definitely worth it.

'You're not married?' He already knew the answer to that. He'd asked Angus before he took the post at the surgery.

She shook her head.

'No boyfriend?'

Again she shook her head. A chilly breeze found their hiding spot and she shivered. 'What about you?'

He didn't miss a beat. 'No, I don't have a boyfriend, either.'

He saw the corners of her mouth twitch, but she quickly checked the impulse and he watched, fascinated, as she forced all expression from her lovely face.

'I was married,' he admitted at last. 'For a short while.'

A very short while. The experience had been the worst mistake of his life. His wife hadn't been able to compete with the memory of the girl Nick had left behind. Very reasonably, she'd demanded a hundred per cent of his attention and he hadn't been able to give it — not when, every time he closed his eyes, it was Emma's face he saw.

Silence greeted his revelation. He thought he glimpsed something in her face for a moment before she resumed her deadpan demeanour and went back on the offensive.

'So why the third degree?'

It seemed she was intent on not entering into conversation about his past.

He grinned. 'Just making sure the coast's clear.'

Expression was back loud and clear, and he winced. She was not happy. The only thing giving him hope she might not, perhaps, be quite as cross as she seemed was that she hadn't turned round and stormed straight back to town.

* * *

He'd been married. She didn't want to probe why she felt stunned by that news. When people had been apart for as long as she and Nick had, it was only natural that other relationships might crop up. So why did the knowledge bite into a dark place in her soul and make her so uneasy?

He sat on the rock only feet away, his slow grin wickedly sexy, completely unaware of the turmoil he stirred within her.

She needed to get a grip. His marriage was none of her business. *He* was none of her business. Emma needed to make sure he understood that.

'You can't seriously imagine I'd want a relationship with you.'

His smile faded and he raked a careless hand through too-long hair, his gaze clinging urgently to her face.

'Why not? After this afternoon, you can't possibly deny there's still an attraction between us.'

'You're too late, Nick. Fourteen years too late, in fact.'

She was shocked at her harsh tone, but she was furious, damn it. All those years she'd longed for him and now when she thought she'd reached a point of equilibrium and acceptance, he was back to wreak havoc with her peace of mind.

'I needed to prove myself before we could have a future.'

Emma shook her head and glanced unseeingly across the valley below. She wasn't buying that. The Nick she'd known wouldn't have stayed away if he'd wanted to be with her.

'I don't believe you.'

'You wanted me to force my way back as a failure? As a nobody, and prove to everyone they were right? That I wasn't good enough for you?'

She shivered in the breeze again. 'That's rubbish. I loved you, you knew I did. I never said — never even thought, not once — that you weren't good enough for me.'

'Maybe you didn't. Everybody else thought it, though. Your mother actually said it.'

Emma was appalled. 'What? When did she say that?'

'After I left Tullibaird I phoned, tried to visit — more than once. And every time I did, she told me you were better off without me. That if I loved you, I should stay away.'

Emma bit into the soft underside of her lip and tasted blood.

'When was this?'

'Does it matter?'

'Maybe it does.' Timing was crucial — and it would very much depend on when he'd attempted to make contact whether she would be able to excuse her mother's very callous behaviour towards Nick.

He sighed. 'It took me a while to get myself together after Mum died. I blamed myself, thought I should have done something to help her. But eventually, I began to pull myself together — to plan a future. It took me about six months and I know that's a long time, but I came back . . . '

'And I wasn't at home.'

Nick was mesmerised by the way the blood drained from Emma's face, leaving her deathly pale. He began to suspect something he hadn't been able to appreciate as a sixteen-year-old — there could have been more to Moira's hostility than an overprotective mother guarding her daughter's well-being.

'Where were you, Emma?' he asked softly.

'I . . . I . . . ' She was still as white as a ghost and shivering slightly in the evening air now. He yearned to draw her into his arms and hold her close — to warm her with heat from his body. But he guessed she needed space.

'Hospital. I was in hospital.'

This was the second time she'd mentioned a hospital stay. Anger flared through him. She'd spent time in hospital and nobody had told him. 'Why were you in hospital?'

There was something dark in her eyes and he wished he hadn't asked. Dread clawed at him with icy fingers. When they'd lain together as teenage sweethearts, she'd sworn she wouldn't be able to live without him. He'd carried her softly spoken declaration in his heart, it had given him validation — if Emma loved him that much, he was a worthy human being.

But what if she'd meant it literally? What if, after he'd been forced to leave without warning, she'd thought she couldn't carry on? Nick felt the sickening force of dread grip his stomach.

'You didn't . . . ' He stopped and cleared his throat.

'What?'

'Emma, after I had to leave . . . you didn't . . . hurt yourself?'

'What?' Her eyes were wide; she seemed to be having trouble processing his words.

There was nothing for it, he had to ask. Had to know.

'Were you in hospital because you'd deliberately caused yourself harm?'

'You mean — ?' Her eyes widened. 'No. No, of course not.'

Relief flooded through him and he heaved in a deep breath. At least that was one thing he could cross off his guilt list. He couldn't help himself, he inched his long fingers towards where hers were resting on the rock — closer until the tips of their fingers were touching.

Emma snatched her hand away and scrambled further up the rock, horrified by the heat that pooled in her tummy without warning.

'Don't, Nick,' she implored.

'Don't what? Are you asking me again not to touch you?'

Her eyes fluttered closed. Looking at him was temptation beyond endurance. He wanted to touch her — and she needed the contact. But she couldn't allow it to happen.

She gave a short nod.

'You can't ask me that.' His voice was close now, his breath fanning her face. 'I need to touch you . . . '

His voice was a whisper in her ear that sent a shock of sensation right down to her toes and the citrus scent of his aftershave, as fresh as a spring morning, assaulted her nostrils and made her feel weak.

'I can't help it, Em. I need to touch you every bit as much as I need to breathe.'

Her eyes fluttered open and she found him gazing, with intent, at her mouth. He was going to kiss her. He moved his broad frame closer, his mouth inches from hers, his breath warm on her face.

She could barely breathe. Her pulse was going haywire — he was going to kiss her . . . and she was going to let him.

The sound of frantic barking and a woman's scream drowned out the pounding sound of her heart. Her head snapped round to look in the direction of the noise, towards the trees and the ravine that cut into the hillside.

Shocked, she turned back to Nick, but he was already running towards the barking dog. She raced after him, her feet thudding against the soft ground at a terrific pace, but she trailed a long way behind and, by the time she reached the edge of the ravine, he was halfway down the sheer, fifty-foot face.

'Are you mad? What are you doing?' she screeched as a chocolate Labrador yelped pitifully after him. It was then she noticed the still body of a woman lying at the foot of the ravine, the stream bubbling over her motionless body. She realised exactly why he'd put himself in that kind of danger.

Mary from the post office — it had to be Mary. This was her dog, Sadie, whining helplessly for her mistress. A sickening grip took hold of her stomach. Mary's body was deathly still. A fall from this height onto rocks . . . well, it didn't look good.

Without giving much thought to it, she launched herself after Nick and scrambled down the narrow gorge, accompanied by a renewed burst of barking. She'd done a bit of climbing in her time, but she'd never descended from this height without a harness before.

Carefully she felt with her toes, searching for a foothold — and, when she found one, she tested her handholds before repeating and continuing her descent. Concentrating, she tried to block out Sadie's howls. The dog would have to wait.

She was half way down when her foot

slipped. Frantically, she scrambled to regain her tenuous hold and her mobile slipped from the pocket of her jeans. Emma snapped her head round just in time to see it smash onto the rocks. She took a deep breath, trying to calm herself — she didn't want to join Mary, and her own shattered mobile, on the floor below.

'Emma.' Nick's voice reached her and calmed her. 'Emma, feel carefully with your toes. There's a narrow ledge about a foot or so below you.'

She did as Nick said and was grateful to find herself balanced on the ledge for a moment while she regained her wits. Realising she had to get moving, however, she continued her descent and soon her foot met with the firm, rocky floor of the ravine. She landed on the ground with a grateful sigh.

Nick was on his knees in the stream, tending to the injured woman.

'Is she — ' Emma's voice was hoarse. She couldn't bring herself to ask if Mary was alive.

'She's unconscious. There's a pulse, but it's very weak.'

'We need to get her out of this water, Nick.' Emma knew it was dangerous to move Mary after her fall, but the fresh mountain stream was very cold; she needed to be pulled out of its grip before the possibility of hypothermia became reality. Together they lifted Mary, taking care to minimise movement of her spine, and placed her on the drier rocks.

'You know this woman?'

Emma nodded. 'She's a patient of mine. Mary Pierce, from the post office. We need to get her to hospital quickly. There's not much we can do without equipment, and her injuries need to be assessed.'

Emma thought longingly of her medical bag — not quite the supplies she needed to treat a fall from such a height as Mary had plunged, but it would have been better than nothing.

'Mary, I'm Dr Rudd. Can you hear me?' They both watched closely for a response. There was none. Nick looked across to Emma. 'We can't risk moving her again without immobilising her. And she'll need to be winched out of here in any case.'

Emma glanced across to where her mobile lay in several pieces. 'Do you have your phone?'

Nick shook his head. 'Afraid not. I don't officially start work until Monday so it wasn't likely anyone would need me.'

'If you'd been a Scout you'd have been prepared.'

He got to his feet, his jeans still dripping water onto the rocks and shrugged a broad shoulder. 'You know me, Em — never was a joiner.' He made to go back the way he'd come.

'Where are you going?'

'To fetch help.'

'But . . . '

He turned, his blue eyes no longer playful. 'I'll be quicker.'

That couldn't be argued with, so she didn't even try. She nodded.

He gave a lop-sided grin that made something flutter in her tummy. 'I'll be back. I promise.' And with that he made his way back up the sheer incline.

'Just don't take another fourteen years,' she muttered under her breath.

* * *

Darkness was fast descending. Mary was showing no signs of movement so Emma quickly checked for a pulse — slow, but still there. Really, she should take those wet clothes off, but she couldn't risk the damage that might be inflicted. Mary had to be kept as still as possible in case there was a spinal injury. Emma shrugged out of her jacket and covered the patient with it as best she could before settling herself on a low rock so she could continue to hold Mary's head in place.

Mary was very lucky she hadn't fallen on one of the sharper rocks that littered the ravine floor, Emma reflected. The situation was bad enough, but it could still have been so much worse.

'Nick won't be long.' She spoke soothingly. Mary wasn't able to respond, but she knew that, sometimes, patients could hear and understand what was being said to them, even when unconscious. 'Just hang on in there, Mary. You'll be okay.'

She glanced at her watch. Five minutes had elapsed since Nick had left them — not quite the longest five minutes of her life, but it was close. 'He'll have made his way out of the trees by now — won't be long before he gets to town.'

Sadie was still barking frantically at the top of the ravine, concerned for her mistress. The noise was driving Emma mad, but there was nothing she could do apart from try to block it out. 'Just a little longer — help will be here soon,' she soothed.

Suddenly Mary groaned and groggily tried to lift her head.

'Take it easy.' Emma increased her hold on Mary's head to stop the movement. 'You need to keep very still. Do you understand me, Mary? It's important. You've taken quite a fall. If you move now, you could cause yourself serious damage.'

Mary murmured something incoherent then groaned again.

'Sadie,' she rasped.

'Sadie's fine. Listen, you can hear her barking.'

A brief smile touched Mary's lips before she lapsed into unconsciousness again. Emma sighed and glanced heavenward. They had to get Mary to hospital soon. She needed scans and X-rays to ascertain the full extent of her injuries. In all probability there would be massive internal injuries and a few broken bones, too.

How long did it take to get back to town, for heaven's sake?

'Nick, where are you?' she muttered with growing urgency. Mary was showing no further signs of regaining consciousness. Her pulse was growing increasingly weak — and she was becoming colder by the second. If help didn't arrive in the next few minutes, it might well be too late.

In reality, it had all taken less than half an hour, but it seemed like forever to Emma as she waited. Then it all happened at once — Nick's return, the helicopter arriving and hovering overhead, unable to land because of the trees, Mary being immobilised and winched out of the gorge . . . And then Emma herself was being winched into the helicopter to accompany Mary to hospital.

Everything was going to be okay.

* * *

Nick stood on the floor of the ravine and watched Emma being lifted over the tree tops and into the Navy Sea King helicopter. She was to accompany Mary so she could hand the patient over to colleagues at the hospital.

Her discarded jacket still lay on the rocks. He picked it up and breathed in her achingly familiar floral scent.

Her last words to him, shouted over the noise of the helicopter, had been about the dog. He was to take Sadie home.

Emma had thought he might leave the dog! He didn't know why he was surprised; he probably deserved her low opinion. If he was honest, he had a low opinion of himself after leaving her the way he had fourteen years ago — and knowing circumstances had forced him away didn't make it any better. He smiled grimly. It was obvious he had a lot of work ahead if there was any hope of regaining the coveted prize of Dr Emma Bradshaw's trust.

The helicopter disappeared from view and the downdraught rustled the treetops as it went. He waited as the noise receded until all that was left to hear was the barking Sadie. It didn't take Nick long to reach the dog — he was an old hand at climbing up and down this way now.

'Come on, girl, let's get you home,'

he said reassuringly. Sadie, pitifully pleased to be taken in hand, trotted at his heels.

'What happened to Mary?' he asked her. 'Did you trip her up? Or did she miss her footing?'

Either way, Sadie's mistress had taken quite a tumble and he could only hope she'd be okay.

He also held the same hope for Emma — that she'd be okay. He knew he'd dropped the news that he'd been married on her with little finesse and even less tact. He'd wondered how he should tell Emma about Mel. He'd rehearsed it, worried over the words to use . . . and in the event he'd blurted it out and they'd been interrupted before he could explain.

He needed to tell her the reason his brief marriage had failed. It had been so totally unfair on Mel, but Nick had convinced himself he had to move on from his obsession with Emma. He'd realised his mistake barely a month into his marriage.

There was nobody home when he dropped by the post office with Sadie. He wished he'd asked Emma if Mary lived alone. For all he knew, there might not be anyone to take the dog.

'Mary's out,' the middle-aged neighbour told him when he knocked at his door. 'Taken the dog up the hill like she does every night.'

As he spoke, the man's confused glance fell on Sadie. Nick introduced himself and explained briefly what had happened.

'She's a widow.' The man dashed Nick's hopes that he would soon be rid of the dog.

'I wonder if I could ask you to take Sadie in, just until other arrangements can be made. I'd take her to my home, but I'm not properly settled yet.'

'No problem, Dr Rudd. Leave her with me. She often squeezes through the fence into my garden anyway, to see my two. I'll happily keep her till Mary comes home, if it'll help.'

Gratefully, Nick headed back to the

small cottage he'd rented in the centre of town, not far from the surgery. If he had brought the dog back here, they'd probably never find her again amongst the piles of boxes and bags containing all his belongings.

It didn't take him long to get changed. It took a little longer to find what he was looking for. And then he was off, into the night, with a roar of his bike.

* * *

Emma rubbed her temple as she stepped outside the hospital and breathed in a lungful of the cool night air. It had been a long day. She'd handed Mary over to hospital staff and then gone to get a cup of coffee while she waited for news. In a minute, she'd have to try to get a taxi to take her home, but she needed some air first.

She ran her hands over her bare arms and wished she'd brought her jacket — it was cold out here.

'How is she?'

She jumped at the unexpected question, the voice reaching out from the shadows. The silhouette of a large man leaning against a motor bike was just visible.

'Nick! You frightened the life out of me. What are you doing here?'

'Wanted to find out how the patient was doing.'

'She's broken several bones and her spleen needs to be removed. I'm only grateful it's not more serious.'

Nick nodded and took a step towards her. It was only then she noticed he was holding something.

'Here — put these on.'

Emma peered suspiciously at the bundle in Nick's outstretched hands. 'What are they?'

She saw the gleam of his teeth as he smiled. 'Protection.'

'Leathers,' she accused.

He shrugged.

'Your *wife's* leathers?' Why did that thought hurt so much?

He shook his head. 'My sister's leathers.'

'Liar. You don't have a sister. There's no way I'm wearing your wife's clothes.'

'She's my ex-wife.' He sighed and used his free hand to comb his hair back from his forehead. 'And these are my half-sister's leathers.'

Emma raised an eyebrow.

'My father had remarried by the time I went to live with him. He and his new wife had a daughter. Lydia. My half-sister.'

His story sounded plausible, but Emma wasn't convinced.

'So why do you have her leathers?'

It was late and she was too cold and too tired to argue, but still she needed answers.

'She didn't like riding the bike as much as she thought she would. I held onto them in case she ever changed her mind. Just put them on, Em — Lydia won't mind if you borrow them.'

He had to be kidding, surely?

'No — thank you.'

'I'm not taking you home on the bike without them.'

She gave a humourless laugh. Did he honestly think she wanted to ride home on that lethal piece of machinery?

'I'm not going anywhere on your bike.'

'Then how do you intend to get home?'

'I'm going to call a cab.'

'Emma.' He pressed the leathers into her arms. 'Put them on. You look dead on your feet. Do you really want to hang around waiting for a cab at this time in the morning? I can have you home and tucked up in bed before it would even turn up.'

He had a point. Damn him.

He reached out and traced the curve of her cheek with his finger. She closed her eyes.

'I'm scared, Nick.' She wasn't only talking about her impending bike ride.

'Nothing to be scared of, Emma,' he promised. 'I'll take care of you.'

She couldn't tell him so, but that frightened her more than anything.

3

Nick exhaled in one long hiss as Emma walked into view. The sight of her slender curves, encased in skin-tight leather, proved she had changed in some subtle ways — she was very much a woman, rather than the girl he'd known before. Did she have any idea how hot she looked? What she was doing to him? Her eyes locked on his as she walked towards him, her gaze unflinching. He swallowed hard as she stopped in front of him.

'Okay, Nick, you've got your way. Now show me what this bike can do.'

A challenge if ever he'd heard one. She pulled her blonde hair back and jammed his spare helmet on before folding her arms across her breasts as she waited for his response. He could feel expectation in the air.

Forcing his body not to react, he

mounted the bike. She slipped behind him, wrapped her arms around his waist, and curved herself around his back. She was so close, he was almost out of his mind. The kick he always got from riding the bike was nothing compared to the high of being so close to Emma. Biting back a curse as the bike roared to life, Nick focused his concentration on the road ahead.

The way home to Tullibaird was clear at this time in the morning — most sensible people were safely tucked up — and they were back at her cottage in record time. He brought the bike to a stop at her gate and took a shuddering breath. She was still curved around his back, her hands closed tight around his waist.

He didn't want to move.

But he knew she had to be at work in a few short hours. She needed to get to bed — alone. No matter what temptations were messing with his head, he couldn't act on them now.

She loosened her hold on him and

climbed off the bike. It was unbelievable how cold he suddenly felt without her. He swung around so he was sitting side on, his legs stretched out either side of her, and took off his crash helmet before helping her out of the one she was wearing.

'So? What did you think of the ride?' His fingers brushed a stray blonde strand from her cheek and she leaned against his hand — just for a moment, but it was enough to let him know she felt the same way he did.

She smiled. 'It was alright.'

He felt the corners of his mouth tug in response. 'Alright enough for you to want to repeat the experience?'

She shrugged. 'Perhaps.'

At least she hadn't told him an outright no. He decided to look on that as encouragement.

'Next time we'll head up the coast,' he promised. 'Now, go to bed, Dr Bradshaw. Go and get some sleep.'

But she lingered, obviously as reluctant to end this as he was. Her even, white teeth bit into the flesh of her lower lip and she looked up at him with such longing that it nearly tore him apart. He had to be strong; he couldn't give in. Not tonight, when they were both already exhausted.

But one kiss goodnight . . . How could he be human and still resist the lush invitation of her lips?

As though reading his mind, she positioned herself between his thighs and leaned, just a fraction, towards him. Her gaze fell on his mouth, the gesture an unmistakable encouragement.

He reached out and his hands very nearly met around her tiny waist. A flick of his wrists and she was sitting on his leg, the globes of her buttocks pressing invitingly against his thigh and her blue eyes huge in the early morning gloom.

Everything he ever wanted was in that face. How could he have stayed away so long? He was an idiot. He knew she'd loved him. Why hadn't he insisted on seeing her when her mother fobbed him off?

He leaned closer. Her breath was warm, her eyes fluttered closed and her lips parted in expectation. She was exquisite.

Who was he trying to kid? He knew why he hadn't forced the issue. It was as he'd told her earlier; everyone had thought he wasn't good enough for her, and he'd known they were right.

'Nick?'

'Yes, Emma.' Blanking out his dark thoughts, he closed the gap between them, touched his lips to hers and something twisted in his gut as he heard her soft moan. Heck, forget being a gentleman and letting her get to sleep — he never wanted to let her go.

* * *

The thrill of riding on his bike, holding him so close it was impossible to know where she stopped and he began, had done something to Emma. Adrenalin, she supposed, mixed undoubtedly with lust. And now, with the touch of his lips on hers, something unfurled deep in her belly. She was feeling things she hadn't come close to experiencing in more than fourteen years. He tasted so good — it had been such a long time, and she wanted him so badly. And yet a doubt nagged at her, warning her to put a stop to this now, before it was too late.

She ignored it.

She liked kissing Nick. She wanted to rip the leathers off his body, to feel his skin next to hers. He'd been the love of her life; kissing him reminded her of the wonderful carefree days they'd spent together. What was the harm in that?

She nearly laughed even as the thought formed. The harm was, she knew exactly where kissing could lead. And she knew the devastation that could result. She'd lived with the heartache every day for years.

He hadn't noticed she'd stopped kissing him back. He was making love to her mouth with such thoroughness, she was nearly out of her mind. But she had to stop him.

'Nick, I can't.' Her voice was muffled against his lips and she pushed at his chest, making him lift his head.

'What's wrong?' He looked dazed and it took all her strength not to kiss him again.

A sob escaped her lips. 'This is all wrong.' She gestured wildly and staggered from his lap. 'We have no business kissing like this.'

She saw confusion in his eyes and wanted to scream. It was all so easy for him — he clearly thought he could just waltz back into her life, and she'd welcome him without a second thought.

'It doesn't feel wrong to me,' he murmured.

Nor did it feel wrong to her. That's what made her so angry. It felt right and good. His arms were where she belonged. But she couldn't go through with it.

He rose to his feet, and she cricked

her neck looking up into his face. Such a beautiful face, and filled with such care and concern for her that she wanted to cry.

A muscle pulsed in his cheek, just as it always had whenever he'd been upset. Her fingers itched to stroke his face, to soothe the errant movement, but she checked herself. He was a predator — any sign of weakness on her part and he'd move in for the kill . . . and she'd welcome him.

As though reading her thoughts, he shook his head.

'Alright, Emma, I won't argue with you now. It's been a traumatic day. You need to get some rest.'

She nodded, grateful he'd chosen not to press the issue.

'Thanks for the lift.'

'Any time.'

She backed up the path, not able to take her eyes from him. Nick had always been her weakness and he was still too gorgeous to be true. Under other circumstances, she'd have dragged him inside.

But her days of taking risks were well over — her previous experience with Nick had made sure of that.

'It's not finished, Emma,' he called as she reached the step. 'Not even close.'

With his promise ringing in her ears, she unlocked the door and bolted inside. She waited until she heard him ride off before she kicked off her shoes and went upstairs.

She had to tell him — soon. Once he knew what had happened, he'd leave her alone. Even he couldn't be heartless enough to pursue this insane path then. He'd understand why she couldn't risk a repetition.

* * *

In her bedroom, she sat on the bed and a sigh racked her entire body. She gravitated towards the photograph in a silver frame on her bedside table. When the midwife had taken the snap, Emma had thought it the worst idea she'd ever heard of.

But now she was grateful for the woman's kindness — she'd understood that Emma would only have her son for a short time and, in years to come, would cherish the reminder. Now that photo was the most precious thing Emma owned — the only photo of the tiny son she'd given birth to.

She hardly recognised herself in the girl gazing down at her baby, and she was shocked anew by how small the baby in her arms was. Lightly she traced her son's image — as still as a doll and as beautiful as a tiny angel.

Nick had a right to know he'd had a son, and Emma was going to have to tell him. It wasn't a conversation she looked forward to. Raking over old wounds was going to hurt them both.

Her mind was still buzzing as she slipped under the covers. Her body was exhausted, but she didn't think she'd be able to sleep — not when she was reliving every moment she'd spent with Nick today . . . and mentally preparing herself for the inevitable reaction when she eventually told him the truth.

She noticed the answering machine was blinking as she was thumping her pillow for the umpteenth time. Another diversion she didn't need — probably her mother. Honestly, why hadn't she put the thing in the living room like a normal person?

Unable to resist, she reached out and pressed the button to retrieve the message.

'Hi Emma — it's Jan. I'll call back tomorrow. Be warned, I'm after a huge favour. And you're allowed to say no.'

Emma settled down and tried to sleep, pretty sure she'd agree to whatever favour her friend was after. She'd head up after work tomorrow so Jan could explain in person. It had been a long time since they'd caught up, in any case, and Emma was going to have to face the situation at some point. Besides, the visit would get her out of town for a couple of days.

* * *

Her weekend away threw up another complication — Jan hadn't been kidding when she'd mentioned a big ask. Even though Emma's first reaction had been to refuse, she'd stamped on her reluctance, pasted on a big smile and assured Jan and Harry she would be happy to help. They would never have made such a request if it hadn't been important.

The time away from Tullibaird had provided a diversion, though, and given her some much needed perspective. She was better prepared now for Nick's presence in the surgery as he started work on Monday morning. At least, that was what she kept telling herself — right up until the moment when she failed to take blood from a patient. She allowed herself three attempts before admitting defeat.

'I'm sorry, Miss Brown, I can't find a vein. Rather than use you as a pin cushion, I'm going to see if a colleague can do better.'

She was well aware that the reason

for her failure to perform this basic procedure was sitting in the consulting room next door. Her mind had been in there with him all morning. It wasn't right — it wasn't professional. She needed to get a grip.

Annie wasn't in the treatment room. Blast. Emma really didn't want to have to ask Miss Brown to come back another day. And she couldn't keep sticking a needle into the elderly woman . . .

She turned and walked out of the room — slap bang into a broad masculine chest.

'Oh, I'm sorry,' she muttered, looking up into Nick's face and reeling back out of harm's way.

'Hello, Emma.' His slow grin had her insides flipping. She struggled for composure and blinked in a completely unsuccessful attempt to ward off the effect of being so close to him. 'I missed you. Where were you this weekend?'

She wanted to tell him it was none of his business, but she couldn't bring herself to do it. 'Staying with my friend, Jan. Er, have you seen Annie? I need her help to take blood from a patient.'

He shook his head and a lock of blond hair fell across his forehead. 'Sorry, I haven't. Can I help?'

Emma chewed her lip. 'It's Miss Brown.'

Nick looked blank. He didn't remember — which was surprising. When he'd been a young boy, Miss Brown had gone out of her way to make Nick's life difficult. 'Our teacher from primary school.' She watched as realisation dawned.

'Let's see if we can get this blood.' Nick walked into the consulting room and drew a chair closer to Miss Brown.

'I'm Doctor Rudd.' He flashed a devastating smile and Emma was surprised to see the old woman positively glow. Nick in charming mode was lethal — and even a crusty spinster like Miss Brown didn't stand a chance.

Nick managed to get the blood sample with little fuss and left Emma to finish the consultation.

'What a nice young man,' Miss Brown remarked as Emma completed forms for the lab. 'It's good that the practice has managed to attract someone of that calibre.'

Emma's eyes narrowed. Their old teacher really had no idea who he was. Although, she flinched momentarily as she realised that she herself hadn't recognised him either at first — and she'd been acquainted with him a darn sight better than Miss Brown ever had.

'He's local — returning to his roots.'

'Really?'

'He was in your class. He used to be Nick Malone.'

Emma waited for the usual expression of disapproval and was pleasantly disappointed when it didn't materialise.

'Oh, I remember him. Bright boy. Always knew he'd do well.'

Emma felt her jaw drop as the teacher made her way from the room. If those sentiments were true, it was a shame Miss Brown hadn't shared them

\with Nick when, as a young boy, he'd desperately needed encouragement. Most likely the woman's head had been turned by a devastating smile. Some people could be so fickle.

Her next patient was no easier to deal with — but for quite different reasons. She'd also known Greg Elder since her schooldays, and he'd always been an oddball. It was a while since he'd been in to see her, though. Following a bit of unpleasantness a few years back, the reception staff had gently encouraged him to see Sandy whenever he'd tried to make an appointment. But now Sandy had retired, he was back to see her.

He shuffled in and refused to make eye contact, but she smiled kindly, nonetheless, trying to put him at his ease. Even though she was anything but comfortable herself in his company.

'I need sleeping tablets,' he demanded gruffly. 'I hardly get a wink of sleep all night.'

'Is there anything troubling you?'

Greg Elder shook his head, while

twisting his hands in his lap. 'Nothing. Just my head buzzing all night. I can't switch off.'

Emma knew of Greg's circumstances — just as she did most of the inhabitants of Tullibaird. She knew he found it difficult to hold down a job. She knew he preferred to roam the town at night, while everyone else slept. And she knew, because his neighbours had told her, that he often slept well into the afternoon.

'I'm reluctant to prescribe sleeping tablets in cases like this,' she told him firmly. 'An adjustment in lifestyle would be much more effective.'

Emma offered advice on healthy living, a change of diet and the benefits of taking proper exercise. 'A bedtime routine is important, too,' she added.

'I need the tablets. I can't sleep at all, it's driving me around the bend.'

'I know sleep deprivation is difficult to deal with,' Emma told him sympathetically. 'Is your bedroom cool, airy and quiet?'

'Yeah,' he snapped.

'Okay. Good. I'd like you to try some relaxation techniques before you go to bed. You need to learn to wind down at the end of the day. And you really need to retire at the same time every night.'

'So you ain't giving me tablets?'

'I'd like you to try my suggestions, first,' Emma persisted. 'And make another appointment to see me in two weeks.'

* * *

'You made quite an impression,' Emma told Nick a little later when she ran into him in the staff room.

He frowned. 'Sorry? I'm not exactly following you.'

'Miss Brown. She's now your number one fan — claims she knew you'd come good in the end. After the way she used to treat you, it makes me so cross.' She spooned instant coffee powder into her mug and poured on hot water.

He shrugged a shoulder. 'Goes with

the territory when you're a doctor. You must have noticed yourself — people don't tend to see further than the medical degree.'

Emma carried her drink over and took the chair opposite him. 'Doesn't it annoy you? She was so horrible to you when you were small. And now she's taking credit for predicting your success.'

'Ah, Em — you know there was only ever one person whose opinion I cared about.'

His stare was intense. Emma squirmed as slow heat suffused her cheeks. She tried to speak — and failed — then cleared her throat and eventually managed to croak, 'Me?'

'Of course, you.'

'Oh.'

'So, Emma.' He leaned across and put his mug down on the table between them. 'What do you think? Has the bad boy turned good?'

Her lips felt dry, her throat parched. She took a long gulp of her still-too-hot coffee and winced as it burned her tongue.

'I never thought you were a bad boy.'

She watched as his blue eyes narrowed. He didn't believe her. He had her marked down as the same sort of judgmental idiot as everyone else. And that hurt her — cut through her defences with an ease that left her reeling.

'Not even when I left you?'

'I don't want to talk about that now. This isn't the time or the place.'

'Then have dinner with me. Tonight. I'll book a table at Giovanni's — we can talk then.'

This was it. The opportunity she'd been waiting for.

'Okay.' She gave a short nod. 'But I'd prefer not to go to a restaurant.' The conversation she had in mind needed to be conducted in private.

'Okay.' He smiled. 'How about you come round to my place? If you're brave enough to risk it, I'll cook.'

A hint of a smile played about her

lips as she watched him hold the door open for Annie as he left the staff room. Emma's smile faded as she noticed the unmistakable look of longing the nurse cast after Nick.

'Oh, but he's just gorgeous. He's wasted here — he should be in films.' Annie was speaking almost to herself, but as she turned and realised Emma was in the room, she flushed a deep red. 'Oh, Emma. I'm so sorry. I didn't mean — '

Emma shook her head. 'Don't worry about it. It doesn't matter.' Even if Annie's open admiration ruptured a jealous streak ten miles wide, she had no rights over Nick. And she hadn't had any for a long time.

'I don't know what I was thinking.' Annie was flustered. 'I mean, everyone knows about you two. Ignore me — no breakfast this morning, it's obviously affected my brain. I'm so sorry, Emma.'

Despite something nasty itching to get out, she forced a smile. 'Nothing to do with me.'

'Oh, but — I mean . . . Aren't you two . . . ?'

'No,' Emma told her quietly. She knew exactly what she was doing. She was giving out the clear message to Annie, and every other single female in Tullibaird, that they were free to chase after Nick with everything they had.

'No, we're not,' she said, this time more certain. 'And we're never likely to be again.'

* * *

Nick was watching out for her later that evening. He'd managed to unpack most of his belongings over the weekend — only two boxes of books remained — and the place was as neat as it was ever likely to be for his guest. A table laid for two in the kitchen, soft lighting lending the living room a cosy glow . . . He wasn't expecting her to be impressed, but it was important she felt comfortable here if she was going to give him the chance to explain what had happened.

He saw her arriving and went to open the door. The first thing he noticed was her hair, swinging loose around her shoulders, the buttercup yellow of her outfit making the gold even more vibrant than usual. Her dress was cinched in at her tiny waist and cut low enough to show the promise of her cleavage. Not that he knew much about dresses, but he approved of this one.

He longed to kiss her, even fleetingly, but held back. The fact she'd agreed to come to his home at all was more than he'd hoped for — he didn't want her to run for the hills before she'd even properly stepped over the threshold. He smiled instead.

'Hi, Em. You look amazing.' He stepped aside to let her in and, as she went past, she stood on tiptoe in her flat shoes and brushed her soft lips against his cheek.

The floral tones of her perfume performed a full assault on his senses and it was all he could do not to take her in his arms, crush her to him and devour her mouth.

Feeling him tense up, she stepped back and looked slightly startled. 'I'm sorry, Nick.'

He took a deep breath. 'I'm not complaining. You can kiss me anytime.'

'I don't know why I did that.'

He hoped it was because she felt kissing him was the natural thing to do, but he needed to put her at her ease. They had a lot to discuss, and he didn't want to complicate matters by over-analysing a friendly greeting.

'Forget it — it was just a peck on the cheek.' A peck that had his heart racing and had left her looking flushed and deliciously flustered. 'Come through and I'll fetch you a drink.'

She settled herself on the sofa and he poured white wine into two glasses before joining her. 'Douglas told me about your father. I'm sorry. He was a good man.'

Her eyes downcast, she nodded. 'Thank you. Yes he was.'

There was silence for a moment before he spoke again.

'It wasn't my choice to leave you fourteen years ago — you know that, don't you?'

He'd always been a man to go straight to the point and there seemed little reason to be any different now.

'I know. Your mother died and you went to live with your dad.'

'We'd made plans to spend our lives together and, if I'd had my way, I'd have stayed here with you.'

She shifted on the sofa and put her glass of barely touched wine down on the side table. 'Nick, you were sixteen, you had little choice in the matter. I know that. But I didn't have an address for you or even a number where I could get hold of you.' She gave a helpless shrug.

He leaned across her, placed his own glass next to hers and gently lifted her hand from her lap. Her skin was pale and so soft. He ran his thumb over the inside of her wrist and heard her soft intake of breath.

'I was always going to come back for you, Em, but I needed to get my head together first. You know why my mum died?'

She nodded. 'It was drink-related.'

'She'd been an alcoholic for years — it eventually took its toll on her body.'

'You couldn't blame yourself for that.'

'I thought I should have been able to stop her — help her.'

'Ah, Nick.' Her arms came around him and he felt he was coming home to where he belonged. She was holding so tight he could barely breathe. Then she eased her grip, held him at arm's length and a fierce light filled her eyes.

'It wasn't your fault. The only one who could have helped your mum was herself. She needed to want to get well before anyone could do anything for her.'

He now knew that to be true, but as a frightened sixteen-year-old boy he'd been convinced he should have been able to do something.

'Whatever I did or said, I couldn't make her stop drinking. And, if I tried, she became violent. That's a tough thing for a kid to come to terms with.'

'Nick? . . . No!' Emma was appalled and it showed. For a moment he wished he hadn't said anything, but he'd come this far. He needed to rebuild his relationship with Emma, and that meant telling her the truth about why he'd stayed away from Tullibaird for months without trying to make contact.

'She hit you?'

He shrugged. 'I was big enough to take it.'

'That's not right. How could she hurt you like that? Why didn't your father help you?'

'They weren't together long. He had no idea she was even pregnant — let alone that I'd been born.'

'Oh.'

'The authorities contacted him after Mum died — it was a shock for him, especially as he was married by then. But he welcomed me — they all did. Dad and my stepmother are both doctors, that's why I decided on a career in medicine.

'It only took a few months of living a normal family life before I realised how dysfunctional things had been when I'd been growing up, and that none of it was my fault. That's when I felt able to come back to you. But you weren't at home, and your mother wouldn't tell me where you were.'

Her glance flickered to the scar on his upper lip.

'You didn't fall against a table?'

Slowly, he shook his head. He'd taken the brunt of his mother's drunken rages for years. By the time he was sixteen, he'd been well over six feet tall and his mother had been nearly a foot shorter, but she'd terrorised him. She'd known there was no way he'd retaliate against her and she'd turned that against him. He'd been powerless. It was humiliating.

But Emma needed to know — to understand why it had been so important for him to get his head together.

She made a muffled sound, her blue eyes darkened and distressed. 'Nick, I had no idea.' She moved closer, leaned towards him and he could feel his heart thumping against his chest. Her face was millimetres away, he could almost taste her kiss on his lips. And then she ran her tongue gently along the length of his scar and the kick of desire nearly knocked him senseless.

'Emma . . . ' He groaned her name, his hands in her hair, holding her to him. 'I need to be with you. Will you stay with me tonight?' And his heart nearly stopped beating completely as he waited for her to answer.

4

She leaned her forehead against his, her arms around his neck. Nick didn't move, hardly dared breathe, as he waited for her response. And then she gave a massive sigh and pulled away. He knew then her answer would be in the negative.

He'd pushed for too much, too soon. He knew there was a lot going on with Emma these days — a lot she seemed reluctant to share. Why hadn't he taken his time? Let her trust him again before urging her back into a physical relationship?

He grimaced, knowing exactly why he'd pushed — he wanted her. He wanted her now every bit as much as he'd ever wanted her. And he had hoped the feeling might be reciprocated.

Emma hated that he'd been hurt, she

wished she could take it all away. But what he was asking . . . it was impossible.

'I can't, Nick,' she murmured, looking away.

But she wanted to. Boy, did she want to. She lifted her gaze to meet his and, even as she willed him to understand, her tummy fluttered with the force of the attraction.

'Please?' His voice was hoarse, cheekbones razor-sharp in the dim light, his eyes boring into her . . . and there, on his cheek, the pulse ticking time away.

She lifted her hand, brushed the back of her fingers against it in a vain attempt to quell the movement.

'I can't sleep with you, Nick.'

'Why not?'

The question hung between them.

Because I can't risk letting you get me pregnant again.

But she couldn't say the words out loud. She hadn't been able to speak to anyone about her baby — not since the day he'd been born. And she couldn't bring herself to tell Nick now. Even though she knew he needed to know.

'I'm — celibate. It's a lifestyle choice I don't wish to reconsider.'

Because if she didn't have sex, she couldn't get pregnant.

'*Celibate?*' A frown of incomprehension appeared on his face. 'I don't understand.'

'Sex complicates things. I just want to be a good doctor and have a quiet life.'

His laugh was harsh. 'You're not serious?'

She gave a humourless smile. 'Nick, I have my reasons. You have to respect that. I won't change my mind. You must know how I still feel about you — I haven't done a very good job of hiding it. If I was going to sleep with anyone, it would be with you.'

Gobsmacked was probably the best way to describe his reaction. The thought ran absurdly through her mind. His jaw dropped and his mouth opened, as though he was preparing for words that didn't come. She couldn't blame him for being surprised. She dealt with people on a daily basis, and for most of those, sex was an integral part of life. Teenagers whose casual attitude to the act of physical love made her wince. Married couples who were unfaithful. Middle-aged and elderly for whom the lack of a sex life was an obsession.

As a GP he must have dealt with the same issues, so for her to hit him with this, without giving him any background to her decision, must be somewhat beyond his comprehension. She knew it was beyond the comprehension of most people.

Heck, even *she* knew her decision was irrational when faced with Nick, her every fantasy packaged neatly in the body of a sex god, asking her to bed. But it was what she'd decided she needed to do. And she couldn't go back on her decision — however strong the temptation.

He rose to his feet and took a couple

of strides to the far side of the room as though he needed to put space between them.

'I don't quite know what to say.'

She smiled again, although there was nothing in the least amusing about the situation. 'I can see that.'

'How long since you last slept with anyone?'

'You've no right to ask me that. It's none of your business.'

'I think it is. I need to understand why you're unwilling to explore what we have here.'

It didn't even occur to Emma to deny they still had something — they were way beyond such silly pretences. Warmth crept up her face as she held his gaze. He deserved an explanation, damn him — he deserved the truth — but she knew she wasn't capable of telling him the whole truth yet.

She took a deep breath before she replied.

'You're the only man I've ever slept with.'

His jaw dropped. 'Really? Fourteen years? How does someone like you stay celibate for fourteen *years?*'

She shrugged. What was she supposed to say? That fourteen years passed by awfully fast when there was a sliver of ice somewhere in your heart? Because it did.

She'd been out with men, of course, but it had never ended well. How could it, when she was only looking for companionship and they always wanted more? Some of them had called her frigid. Some had been a whole lot nastier. In the end, her reputation preceded her and men had stopped asking her out, which suited her just fine.

'I've been busy,' she told him.

She'd been an emotional wreck for a long time. Then her studies had consumed her — offered her a diversion. Her way of life had become a habit all too easily. Fourteen years could fly by quickly — and it was no hardship to remain celibate if temptation didn't wander her way.

But now temptation had hurled itself in her path and she was trembling with the effort of resisting. Nick was . . . well, he was Nick. And she ached for him.

He raked his fingers through his overlong hair. 'Hell's bells, Em. No healthy adult goes without for fourteen years.'

She shrugged. 'Some of us do.'

He didn't answer but continued to stare and she felt distinctly uncomfortable as the quiet grew. She knew that if she was able to talk to him about Nicholas he'd understand her decision, and she wished she knew how to start.

'What happened with us — well, it all affected me quite badly. I don't want to live through anything like that ever again.'

Still he didn't speak.

The quiet stretched. As far as she was concerned, an awkward silence was like a vacuum — it needed to be filled. She cleared her throat. 'I know it must be hard for you to understand — after all, you got over me enough to marry someone else.'

'No.' He was instantly on his knees on the floor in front of her, his hands taking hold of hers, and urgency in his gaze.

'I never got over you, Em. Don't think that. I married Mel because I thought it was time to move on, that your mother was right, that I wasn't good enough for you.'

'And now?'

'I still don't think I'm good enough for you. But I'm working on it. You were always the princess, the unattainable. The fact you were my friend, my lover, made me hope I could be worthy of you.'

'Nick — ' She averted her gaze from his face, unable to process the intensity she saw there. 'You make me sound like the worst sort of snob. And you know I wasn't. I thought I was the lucky one to be with you.'

He laughed softly. 'Don't be daft.'

'You were the most beautiful boy I'd

ever seen.' She gave in to the urge to touch and reached out yearningly to stroke his cheek. 'Being with you, making love with you, made me feel so lucky and so alive.'

'So you were only after me for my body?' he teased and she grinned in response, relieved the mood had lifted. He turned his face and grazed her palm with his lips. 'Mel was a mistake. I married her when I was eighteen — barely old enough to choose what socks to wear. I was still stinging from the things your mother had said, thought perhaps she was right and I should move on.'

'I'm not excusing the things Mum said to you — and it was unforgivable she didn't let us see each other — but it was a difficult time for everyone. On top of everything else, Dad was seriously ill. Mum had a lot of worries and was only trying to protect me.' Emma bit painfully on her lower lip. 'But she was very wrong — I needed you. If I'd known you'd come back, if we'd been able to see each other then, things might be . . . different between us now.'

She'd needed him so much and her mother must have known that. She'd needed his strength and his courage — and his love.

'Emma, I'm sorry I hurt you so badly.'

Tears stung at the back of her eyes. She couldn't speak so she made an incoherent squawk.

'I should have fought for you back then. That's something I'll regret forever. We can't get those years back, but there must be a chance, surely, we can build something for the future together?'

She realised the sobbing sound was coming from her and she despised her own weakness. She needed to tell him about their baby . . . then he'd realise why she couldn't contemplate a future with him. And why she was living half a life — she was still in mourning.

When she couldn't answer, he got to

his feet and pulled her up from the sofa, wrapped his arms around her and drew her into the safety of his broad frame. She breathed in his unique scent and buried her face in his chest, relishing his warmth.

Being near him calmed her, his strength soothed her and, eventually, she managed to regain some sort of composure.

She sniffled. 'I've got your shirt wet.'

'It'll dry.' Still enveloping her in his arms, he brought his face down to hers and gently kissed the tears from her cheeks. 'All I seem to do is make you cry.'

The touch of his lips on her face sent an electric reaction all the way to her toes. A tremor ran through her and she drew in a shaky breath. 'It's not your fault, Nick. I need to toughen up.'

He shook his head. 'No, you don't. You're perfect as you are. Now, dry those tears.'

She sniffed and forced herself to smile. 'I'm okay.'

'Good.' Releasing her from the comfort of his embrace, he led her through to the kitchen. 'Come on, let's eat.'

The last thing she felt like was food, but when Nick had gone to the trouble to cook for her, she couldn't leave without eating. He pulled out a chair for her at the tiny kitchen table and she sat while he went to the oven.

'Any news about Mary Pierce?' Nick heaped servings of lasagne onto plates and placed one in front of her, before folding his large frame into his own chair. It was a snug fit. These cottages weren't the biggest, and Nick's kitchen was tiny. His knees touched hers beneath the table — she wondered, absurdly, what his reaction might be if she reached over and grazed her hands over his thighs.

She swallowed hard and took an unusual interest in her plate — scared to look at him in case he read her mind and realised she was thinking of molesting him.

'I phoned to check before I left the surgery this evening. She's going to be okay, but will be in hospital for a while yet.'

'She's a lucky lady.'

'Very lucky.' She took a forkful of lasagne, risked a glance and immediately wished she hadn't. Just looking at him had her heart racing, without the added distraction of his knee pressed against hers. 'When you think what could have happened if we hadn't been up there when she fell . . . '

'But we *were* there.' His voice was firm and she realised he was right — there was no point in considering the worst case scenario. She knew that — had learned a long time ago not to waste her time on 'what if's.

'I thought I might visit tomorrow evening. Would you like to come with me? After all, if it wasn't for you, things would have been much worse. Not that I expect she'll be in any fit state to entertain visitors, but I want to see her for myself. And I hate thinking of a patient of mine being so far from home with nobody going to see them.'

She was babbling — she sounded like a ninny. But she didn't want him to think she was asking him on a date — not when there wasn't any prospect of a future. There couldn't be a future for her with Nick — not with the way she felt about intimacy. A man like Nick needed a full relationship. Even if he didn't, she would drive herself mad, wanting to touch him and knowing she had to keep her hands to herself.

'That's a good idea. Of course I'll come.'

It was getting dark when Emma made noises about going home. She was surprised when he offered to come with her.

'There's no need. I'll be perfectly fine on my own.'

'It's late — I want to make sure you get home safely.'

She laughed, but appreciated the thought. It was nice that he was worried about her. 'The crime rate in Tullibaird is still practically zero.'

'I know, but I'd still like to see you home just the same. So, indulge me?'

Faced with the prospect of an argument or of spending a few minutes longer in his company, there really wasn't a contest. She said no more — her silence signifying her agreement. He pulled the front door closed behind them and walked towards the gate.

They were barely out onto the street when someone rushed past them — a man, dressed in dark clothing. He didn't stop and didn't offer a greeting. She saw Nick raise a surprised eyebrow. Everyone in Tullibaird stopped to say hello — if only because it was a way to find out what was going on.

'Greg Elder,' she explained and was met with a blank look. 'He was the year above us at school. He was always a bit eccentric,' she continued, trying to trigger Nick's memory. 'In fact, he's still a bit eccentric, but he's harmless.'

She hadn't forgotten how uncomfortable she'd felt in his company at the surgery earlier but, otherwise, she no longer had any reason to believe he wasn't as innocuous as everyone claimed.

Greg Elder disappeared around the corner and Emma was glad. Harmless or not, he still made her feel uneasy.

Much more pleasant was Mary Pierce's neighbour, Dougal MacDonald, who was now walking towards them, a friendly smile firmly in place.

'Busy around here tonight,' Nick murmured in Emma's ear before returning the man's smile.

It was obvious Dougal had been out for a late evening walk with the dogs — his own and Sadie — and all were excitedly greeting them with barks. 'Evening, doctors,' he called as he approached.

'Hello,' Emma and Nick answered at the same time.

'Any news on Mary?'

'Doing fine,' Emma supplied. 'It will take a while before she's home, but they expect her to make a full recovery.'

'Good, good.' With that he turned to Nick. 'I'm glad I bumped into you, Dr Rudd. I was wanting to thank you for the dog food you dropped by. Very generous. That lot is enough to feed an army of dogs for a year.'

Nick grinned. 'Least I could do. It was kind of you to agree to take Sadie in. Mrs Pierce will be relieved to know her dog's in good hands.'

They walked on and Emma couldn't help smiling as they neared her house.

'What?' Nick demanded.

'Nothing.'

'It must be something. That's the biggest smile I've seen on your face since I got back.'

She laughed. 'I was just thinking, the bad boy's just a softie at heart. It was very thoughtful of you to send dog food to Dougal.'

He grinned in reply and took hold of her hand, drawing her towards him and pulling her tight against his body. She relished being crushed against him. In the safety of the main street, she knew there would be no pressure on her and, with that knowledge, a sizzle of awareness rippled down her spine.

'I've a good mind to make you pay for laughing at me, Dr Bradshaw.'

She was breathless as his blue eyes fixed on her mouth. 'What did you have in mind, Dr Rudd?'

'You don't have any rules against kissing?'

'I don't.' She shook her head. 'Although I hardly think it would be seemly for two of the town's GPs to be seen snogging in public.'

'I have a solution to that objection.' He reached down and took her door keys from her fingers and, still holding onto her hand, he tugged her gently towards the house.

He pulled her indoors, kicked the front door closed, and braced his hands on the wall on either side of her head. She was effectively trapped, but now she'd confided one of her secrets, she knew he wouldn't let things go too far. A repeat of what had happened when they'd been sixteen wasn't on the agenda. Even if she didn't entirely trust herself around him, she trusted him. He was decent and honourable — so knowing that he'd respect her lifestyle choice was a given. It would go no further than kissing.

And kissing, she could handle. Kissing she liked.

Specifically, she liked kissing Nick.

Her eyes fixed on his mouth. 'Bring it on,' she invited, her voice husky even to her own ears. She was rewarded with a slow grin that had her insides quivering and he lowered his head slowly, so slowly, towards hers . . .

Yet she wasn't prepared for the sensations unleashed by his mouth on hers. This was unlike any other kiss they'd ever shared — when he slipped his tongue between her parted lips, the resulting explosion of passion had her moaning softly and clawing at his clothes.

Nick gasped as her cool hands slipped beneath his shirt and stroked the bare skin of his back.

This was a bad idea. He knew he had to stop it now, before things got out of hand. She'd trusted him enough to tell him she didn't do sex any longer and, whatever his personal view of this information, however much he wanted to seduce her into changing her mind, he had to respect her wishes. He didn't want to take advantage of her; she'd only hate him.

He groaned against her mouth as her hands moved over his body. It would be the easiest thing in the world to carry her up to bed now — he wasn't daft, he knew she still wanted him. But before they made love again, she had to make a conscious decision that it was the right thing.

He had no doubts at all that they would end up in bed — and soon. Nobody serious about staying celibate would kiss him in the way she was doing now.

Her lips were on his neck now, her breath hot against his skin. 'You taste so good,' she murmured against him, all the while raining tiny kisses that were driving him slowly out of his mind.

He closed his eyes and groaned again. He didn't want to stop this. He needed it to reach its natural conclusion.

Nick took his hands from the wall and lightly ran them down her back before reaching down to cup her bottom and lift her up. She shuddered against him, nearly pushing him over the edge. It would be so easy to allow this wave of passion to carry them both along, all the way . . .

But he wanted a relationship with her more than he wanted a quick fling. He'd planned a future with her when they'd been sixteen, and just this brief re-acquaintance had proved to him nothing had changed in that respect. He wanted it all — marriage, children, everything they'd talked about as teenagers.

She'd changed in the time he'd been away, though. He needed to know why, but he was slowly being driven beyond the point of coherent thought. She'd unbuttoned his shirt now — her lips caressing his chest. She was completely out of control, her eyes glazed, her face flushed.

With a tortured expletive, he let go his hold of her and let her slide down his body to her feet. Then he forced himself to take a step back.

Deprived of his support, she leaned back against the wall — as though her legs refused to hold her. He knew the feeling; his own limbs were decidedly dodgy.

'Em, I'm going to leave now. I'll see you in the morning.'

He closed his eyes momentarily against the invitation in her blue eyes and the sight of her swollen, parted lips. The temptation to kiss her once more was unbearable, but he knew that if he did, he wouldn't be leaving any time soon.

With a racking sigh, he turned away before opening his eyes. He crashed through the door into the night with a mumbled, 'Night, Em.'

* * *

Emma stared at the door, unable to move, for a long time. So many disturbing thoughts raced through her brain. Uppermost was the knowledge that she needed to cultivate a healthy amount of self-control around Nick. She couldn't keep her hands off him — and it wasn't fair to either of them.

Desperate need gnawed deep inside her. She hated herself for that — hated that she couldn't kill her need for his body stone dead, as she needed to. She had no business losing control the way she did around Nick. She was an adult and a doctor; she knew exactly where that sort of behaviour could lead. And she knew only too well the devastation the results could still cause — whatever precautions were taken.

Tonight hadn't gone as well as she'd hoped. She should never have agreed to go to his house. But she'd thought it would be easier to tell him if they were on their own.

And yet she still hadn't told him about their baby.

The knowledge that his own father had been ignorant of Nick's existence had added another dimension. History had repeated itself, but whereas Nick had managed to grow to the brink of adulthood before he'd met his father, Nicholas hadn't been given that chance.

When she did manage to find the words to tell him the truth, he was going to hate her. Whether he'd blame her for what happened as much as she blamed herself remained to be seen. But she was certain that the longer she left it, the stronger his hatred would be.

Maybe it would solve her immediate problem, because he was sure to leave her alone once he found out.

Yet the thought of Nick hating her hurt terribly.

5

'Good morning, Dr Bradshaw.' Mrs Cullen was Emma's first patient of the day.

Emma smiled in welcome although, knowing recent family events that had unfolded within the Cullen family, apprehension settled over her like a dark cloud.

'Take a seat,' she invited, trying for a bright and businesslike tone as her sense of foreboding increased.

'I asked to see you, especially.' Mrs Cullen took her hanky from her pocket and wiped her eyes. 'I know you're the only doctor here who can begin to understand what I'm going through.'

Emma just about stopped her shoulders from slumping. Every now and then this would happen. A patient who had suffered a bereavement would come to her, expecting empathy — and a prescription for something to dull the pain. They had her down as an easy mark because they knew she was still grieving herself. Emma's own pain called out to them like a beacon.

In truth, every doctor here had lived through the loss of someone close, but Emma wasn't about to point that out — not when Mrs Cullen was obviously upset.

'What you're going through is normal.' Emma touched the patient's arm. 'All part of the grieving process.'

'But it's been six months now. Tell me, does it get any easier?'

She only just stopped herself drawing a sharp breath. She hated it when people referred to Nicholas, even when the reference was as veiled as this. It was an intrusion.

'Obviously I haven't lost a husband of fifty years, as you did.' She took a deep breath. 'From my own experience, you find ways to live with grief, but it never goes away.'

'Have you really found a way to live with it?'

Emma shrugged a shoulder and gave a weak smile. She needed to deflect this fast. She'd already said too much. She was not going to have this conversation with a patient. Even if she could find words to talk about her son, she still wouldn't want to discuss him with a patient.

'People do find ways, Mrs Cullen. It's part of the human condition to carry on.'

'I see Nick Malone's back,' Mrs Cullen continued. 'That can't be easy for you — seeing him again will remind you.'

'Dr Rudd,' she corrected automatically. 'Nick's surname is Rudd now.'

Mrs Cullen nodded. 'So I heard. Seems to me he's hiding from the past, too, changing his name like that. Of course, losing Nicholas will have been difficult for him, as well. People forget it's hard for the father — losing a baby.'

Emma felt her face flame — it was

definitely time to deflect the conversation. 'Mrs Cullen, I could refer you to a grief counsellor, if you'd like.'

'Good heavens, no need for that, dear. Like you, I'll have to find a way to live with it.' Mrs Cullen got to her feet. 'I just need to talk about him, sometimes, that's all. I'll maybe make another appointment and come back to see you soon.'

'Goodbye, Mrs Cullen,' she replied through numb lips as her head began to throb merrily behind her eyeballs.

She took a few minutes before calling for her next patient. This was as close as she'd ever been to talking about what happened. Her mother had tried to get her to discuss it, of course. She'd even tried to persuade her to accept counselling, but the only way she'd been able to cope had been to remain silent. If she didn't speak about it, then she could hug the experience close — because, however horrible the aftermath, the brief time she'd spent with Nicholas had also been wonderful. Because those moments had been so brief, she needed to keep them for herself.

Nevertheless, she did need to learn to talk about Nicholas. Because very soon she'd have to share him with Nick.

Even while she was upsetting her through referring to Nicholas, Mrs Cullen had rammed home just how unfair she was being to Nick. The townspeople had long memories and Nick's return would, she knew, have brought thoughts of Nicholas and the trauma surrounding that time back into their collective consciousness. If Nick meant as much to her as she knew he did, she had to tell him . . . before someone else did.

When he'd revealed last night that Angus had told him about her dad, she'd nearly passed out. In fact, if she'd believed such a thing possible, she would have said her heart had stopped beating for just a moment. Then she'd realised he would not have been so calm if he'd been told about Nicholas, too.

At that moment, though, she'd acknowledged how much she would hate for him to find out from someone else. It was her job — her duty and her responsibility — to tell him.

She had to be grateful that nobody had revealed the truth yet. But the townspeople did gossip; it was only a matter of time. Her conversation with Mrs Cullen had underlined that. Even if they didn't mean to cause deliberate trouble, they might assume that Nick knew, and find a reason to mention Nicholas to him.

She glanced at her computer screen and sighed as she noticed the name of her next patient: Alexandra West. Alexandra was a lovely girl — it was her date of birth that always caused Emma upset. Seeing the teenager on her list, she was reminded yet again of the teenager Nicholas would have grown into . . . for he and Alexandra had been born on the same day.

It seemed that all the signs were intent on reminding her about how unfair she was being to Nick. Not that he was ever out of her thoughts . . . but today there were powerful reminders of Nicholas at every turn.

She forced a smile as her young patient entered the consulting room with her mum.

Angela West had been good to Emma over the years. They had become acquainted when they'd both been pregnant. Although ten years older, the other woman had made a point of befriending Emma. When the entire village had been pointing a collective accusatory finger, Angela had offered the hand of friendship and Emma could never forget such a kindness.

Angela's pregnancy had been a few months further advanced — Alexandra had been born at full term — so she'd been able to reassure Emma whenever she'd been worried. Angela's attitude had made a refreshing change for Emma from the sly glances and the whispering behind her back. Not to mention the frosty atmosphere she'd had to endure at home when her mother wasn't at the hospital with Emma's father.

'Good morning, Alexandra.' Emma made sure to include both daughter and mother in her smile. 'Take a seat. And Mum can sit here.' She pulled a second chair around and once everyone was seated, she relaxed back in her own chair. 'Now, how can I help you this morning?'

'We're a bit concerned about a mole on Alexandra's tummy,' Angela explained. 'It's been bleeding a little bit. I think it may be that the zip on her jeans is rubbing against it, but we thought we should ask you what you think — just to make sure.'

'You did the right thing. It's always best to get these things checked out. Okay, Alexandra, if you'd like to hop onto the table, I'll take a look.'

The mole was exactly on the line where Alexandra's zip would catch it, so in all probability, Angela was right about the cause of the bleeding.

Looking closer, Emma saw there were no irregularities on the blemish itself and the edges were smooth, the colour even — apart from the tiny nick where it had obviously been aggravated by Alexandra's clothing.

'Any itching, or bleeding that might not be a result of rubbing against the zip?'

The patient shook her head. 'No, Dr Bradshaw.'

'Has it grown at all recently? Or changed colour?'

Alexandra shook her head again. 'No. Not that I've noticed.'

'Okay.' Emma went over to the sink and washed her hands. 'It looks like nothing to worry about, but it does seem to be a nuisance if it's catching on your clothing.' She took a handful of paper towels from the dispenser and dried her hands. 'I'm going to ask one of my colleagues, Dr Rudd, to have a quick look. He can give us a second opinion. He's planning to start the minor surgery clinic up again, so he can speak to you about removal.'

She didn't want to call Nick in for so many reasons — all to do with her own state of mind. But her duty was to Alexandra.

She caught him between patients. 'Sure, I'll have a look,' he agreed and he followed her into her consulting room.

Emma bit her lip as she watched from the far side of the room as he examined the patient. Seeing Nick so at ease with the youngster, making her laugh, explaining the procedure, made her realise he would have been a terrific dad for Nicholas.

It was unbearably poignant. Nick was treating this youngster with absolutely no idea that he should have had a son exactly the same age.

Nick explained the procedure for removal. 'It's entirely up to you,' he said. 'But if you decide to go ahead, you can book an appointment for my clinic.'

Alexandra looked at her mother. 'I think I'd like it removed.'

Angela nodded. 'Okay — maybe we

can make an appointment on the way out.'

* * *

She managed to keep her bright and breezy facade in place throughout the consultation. But, once she was alone, Emma deflated back onto her chair. She was so suddenly weary, she didn't think she could feel worse if she'd gone ten rounds with a heavyweight champion.

Luckily, her morning surgery was a busy one and she was forced to keep occupied as she dealt with a variety of routine problems.

Nicholas was always in her thoughts — as he always was — but, because of today's reminders, those thoughts were more persistent than usual. It all took its toll and she was emotionally exhausted by the time her last patient left.

She was tempted to settle for a sandwich in the staff room before embarking on her home visits, but realised that might bring her face to face with the living, breathing reminder of her past. She decided to go home for lunch, as she did most days.

Mistake number one was not checking to see where her mother was before she left the surgery. Mistake number two; not making a run for it when she smelled bacon cooking in her kitchen. It was a while since her mother had come over to make her a bacon sandwich — or anything else for that matter — at lunchtime. Why today, of all days?

The answer presented itself when Moira rounded on her as soon as she walked into the kitchen.

'Emma — how *could* you?'

One of those very gossips who was, in all probability, angling to get to Nick, had told her mother that Emma had been to his house for dinner last night. Nothing else could account for the look of disgust on Moira's face.

Emma feigned innocence. 'How

could I what, Mum?'

'You spent the night with him.'

She hadn't been expecting that. The accusation hung in the air between them. Emma flushed a guilty-as-charged pink — despite the fact she was completely innocent of the accusation. Her mother had gripped the wrong end of the stick and was now running amok with it.

Moira threw the loaf she was holding down onto the counter so she could give her undivided attention to the task of glaring at her daughter.

Emma stared back, hands on hips. She could have put it right so easily, but she needed to get another point across first. She needed Moira to understand this near-obsessive involvement in her daughter's life was way beyond what was natural or healthy.

'I'm a grown woman. Where I spend my nights — and with whom — is none of your business.'

'I'm your mother; of course it's my business.'

'I'm allowed a life of my own.'

Moira shook her head. 'But you don't *have* a life. I don't understand it. You could have been married with a family by now, if you'd given yourself a chance. You've turned down any decent man who's been near you. Yet, as soon as he's back, you throw yourself at him.'

Emma flinched; she couldn't help it. For all that her mother was angrily hurling words that would hurt, this accusation had hit a bull's eye — she had thrown herself at him last night. And it hadn't been the first time.

'For your information, I didn't spend the night with him.'

Moira picked up the loaf and pointed it with an expression of pure, incredulous fury. 'He was seen coming into your house late last night.'

'Typical small-town mentality.' She rolled her eyes in frustration. 'A man was seen going into a single woman's home after dark, and it was automatically assumed they spent the night shagging each other's brains out.'

'*Emma!*' Moira's eyes widened in shock and the bread fell from her hand onto the floor.

'Well, you started it — listening to the nasty-minded gossips and accusing me of all sorts without checking your facts.' It wasn't even worth guessing which neighbour had reported this event to her mother — it could have been any of them. 'He didn't stay the night. He saw me home, he came in for a minute — and then he went away. But, even if he *had* stayed, it would be nobody's business but mine and his.'

Moira wasn't listening. 'All those nice, eligible men who've asked you out over the years . . . ' In full rant mode, she was spectacularly scary. And Emma had never seen her mother quite this angry before, but still she refused to cower and she refused to apologise.

'I didn't want any of them.' She spoke quietly, reasonably — even though she wanted to shout. Her mother was prone to asthma attacks when under stress and, however angry

Emma might be, she didn't want to make matters worse.

'But you want *him*?' Moira's tone, in contrast, had reached incredulous screech level.

'Yes, I do.'

Moira slammed her hand down on the counter. 'Unbelievable.'

Emma bit her lip before asking, 'How is it unbelievable?'

'All those years, Emma! You've wasted half your life waiting for him.'

'Surely you can understand that. You've chosen to be on your own since Dad died.'

The sudden pallor of her mother's face showed Emma had hit home. But she was too upset to care. She had to say something. She couldn't carry on living like this — allowing her mother to be so nasty about Nick.

'Not the same thing,' Moira insisted. 'I might not be interested in meeting someone else, but that's because I've met the love of my life — and had a child.'

Emma didn't hesitate. 'I've done those things, too.'

Moira had the good grace to go even paler. 'Not the same thing,' she repeated.

'No? Nick is the love of my life. I gave birth to his child — a baby I still love more than anything. How is that different to the way you say you feel about Dad and me? Why do you refuse to accept I love Nick?'

'*Love?*' Moira was appalled and it showed. 'You still think you love him? Even after all that's happened?'

She shook her head. 'No. I don't *think* I love him, Mum. I know I love him.'

She'd never stopped. She realised it now. For all she'd tried to deny it to herself, she'd loved him practically all her life — even for every minute of the fourteen years he'd been away.

Moira leaned over and braced her hands on the work surface, shaking her head.

'You're wasting your life. He's always been a waste of space — just like his mother was. He'll never be anything different.'

Emma felt sick. This unwarranted attack on Nick was unfair in the extreme. He'd never done anything wrong. He'd spent his childhood paying for the sins of his feckless mother and bearing the brunt of the community's disapproval . . . and it was still happening.

'That's not fair, Mum. What has Nick ever done — apart from love me?'

'He killed your father.'

Emma hadn't been expecting that. From somewhere dark and deep, laughter began to bubble. It was inappropriate but, despite the highly emotional sparks flying back and forth in her kitchen, she could still recognise that assertion as the most ridiculous thing her mother had ever said. That was saying something because her mother could be queen of the ridiculous comment.

'Nick didn't kill Dad — the cancer did that.'

'That boy got you pregnant and broke your father's heart. He might have been able to fight his illness if he hadn't used up all his energies on worrying about you. I hold Nick Malone entirely responsible for every bad thing that's happened to our family.'

Emma sat down at the kitchen table.

'This is seriously doing my head in.'

'You should've thought of that before you went running back to that boy. But that's you all over. You never think of the consequences. This time you've gone too far. Your father would be horrified if he knew — I'm so ashamed of you.'

Emma wasn't sure whether her mother believed this nonsense or if she was simply lashing out because she was angry. She struggled to regain some composure as she thought about how to respond.

Her father had been the loveliest man — kind and gentle. He was the first person Emma confided in when she'd discovered she was expecting. She knew Moira was still hurt by that.

She swallowed back the urge to cry and took a deep breath.

'Firstly, it wasn't just Nick to blame for me being pregnant. We were both involved and I was every bit as responsible for my condition as he was. Secondly, once Dad got over the shock, he was really looking forward to Nicholas being born.'

'So was I — and because I was at your father's bedside, I didn't even get to hold the only grandchild I'm ever likely to have. Unless you have a change of heart.'

Way to lay the guilt on, Mum. Emma closed her eyes against the accusation in her mother's face.

'I'm not going to change my mind. I'm never going to have another baby. Not with Nick — nor with anyone else.'

'Well! I should hope not with Nick. Not when there are respectable men who'd be happy to marry you.'

'Nick is respectable.'

'He might be a doctor now, but he's still a Malone. The Malone who left you . . . '

Emma's eyes glinted.

'He came back, though, Mum. Didn't he? While I was in hospital, he came to the house and asked to see me. But you chose not to pass on his messages, or to tell him where I was.'

Moira cringed visibly at Emma's accusation, but at least she didn't try to deny it.

'I did that to protect you. You were better off without him.'

'Don't you think that should have been for me to decide?'

'I thought I was doing the right thing.'

Emma knew that. She knew her mother had only been looking out for her — but she'd been so misguided. There was no way she could bring herself to console Moira now.

'I was still pregnant when he first came back, wasn't I?' She waited a moment and her mother's guilty expression confirmed it was true. 'Didn't it occur to you Nick had a right to know?'

'I should have told him,' Moira said spitefully. 'That would have made sure he'd run for the hills and never come back.'

'Nick would have supported me if he'd known.'

Moira's laugh was chilling.

'Yes, well — we'll never know, will we?'

'And didn't you think Nicholas had a right to be loved by his father? You didn't just cheat me and Nick out of our future — you were also unfair to your grandson.'

Moira looked away and, absurdly, her glance fixed on the hob.

'The bacon's burnt.'

That was the least of Emma's problems.

'I'm not hungry,' she said dismissively. She needed to get Moira out of here — before she worked herself up even further, and made herself ill.

'Look, Mum, I'm really not in the mood for this right now. If you stay, I'm going to say something I'll seriously regret. For both our sakes, I think you should leave.'

If she hadn't been so angry, Emma would have laughed hysterically at the expression of outrage crossing Moira's face.

'If that's how you feel. Just remember I'll be here to put you back together when he lets you down. Just like he did last time.'

She collected her jacket and handbag before slamming the door on the way out.

The smell of the burnt bacon was making Emma feel ill. After packaging it up in tinfoil and putting it in the bin, she sat back at the table and put her hands over her face. Moira's fury had been so intense, she hadn't even registered that Emma had talked about her baby. But the significance wasn't lost on Emma.

She'd spoken about Nicholas and the world hadn't ended. The hurt hadn't gone away . . . but neither had it intensified. She could do this. For the first time, she began to believe she would find the strength to tell Nick about their son.

Her relationship with her mother, though, was heading for a state of no repair. She was still trembling from the volley of blame and wild accusations.

Despite the angry words they'd exchanged, feelings of guilt overwhelmed her. She shouldn't have fallen out with Moira — not when she'd offered Emma so much support in so many ways. It was just a shame that the support was attached to a domineering need to be involved in every aspect of her daughter's life . . . and an irrational hatred of Nick.

How in the name of heaven was Emma supposed to forgive the way her mother had behaved towards Nick fourteen years ago? For the way she continued to speak about him, and the resentment she still harboured?

Nick had been right; there was no way they could get those years back.

And now she knew Nick had come back for her, the pain that sliced through her was unbearable.

In all probability, Nick being with her would not have saved their baby. The doctors had assured her nothing would have done that. But sharing her grief with the person she loved might have saved her from the breakdown that followed.

More than anything, she wished there was some way she could move forward. That she could find some way of having the normal life she'd planned with Nick when they'd been teenagers. But she couldn't see that happening. It was too late — she'd spent too many years so damaged by the past that she couldn't contemplate any kind of future.

Nick didn't deserve some kind of half-woman — he needed someone who could love him physically as well as emotionally. He needed someone who would be able to give him children and the happy family he'd missed out on as he grew up.

Not someone with ice in her heart.

However much she still loved Nick, she was realistic enough to know that she could never be that woman.

She had to let him go.

* * *

These days, Nick liked to think of himself as being decisive and direct. And those qualities, he hoped, went towards making him the kind of doctor he wanted to be. But now, with a few minutes to spare after his home visits, he stood on the road that ran past Moira Bradshaw's house and experienced a slight crisis. Decisive and direct had been replaced by hesitant and uncertain. What he was about to do might go down in history as the most idiotic thing ever done by anyone, ever. And, if it backfired — if Emma thought he'd gone behind her back — then there really would be no hope.

It had to be worth the risk. He needed answers and, with Emma incapable of sharing whatever it was she needed to tell him, maybe her mother might be able to enlighten him. Because he very much feared that the longer it went on, the harder it would be for her.

Yet still he hesitated instead of knocking on the door.

Even greater than the worry that Emma wouldn't approve was the fear of the unknown. Did he really want to find out the secret that was so terrible that it had driven Emma to retreat from normal life for the past fourteen years?

The door creaked open and Moira stepped out onto the doorstep. 'What do *you* want, Nick Malone?'

'It's good to see you, too,' he muttered under his breath and then, louder, 'Hello, Moira.'

'What do you want?' she asked again, more harshly.

'To talk to you.'

She glanced around furtively. 'You'd better come in. I don't want you causing a scene out here where my neighbours can hear. Emma and I will have to live here after you disappear again.'

'I've no intention of causing a scene,' he told her as he followed her inside. 'Besides, I'm here to stay. Whether you like it or not.' It was funny how seeing this woman, facing the same kind of hostility as he had done as a child, brought out the same immature responses. He was better than that now. He had to remember he had outgrown his belligerent youthful ways.

The look she threw him left no doubt she did not like it. If she wasn't Emma's mother he wouldn't have been concerned, but he didn't want to be the cause of a family rift. He didn't want Emma to have to choose between them, so he would need to drop his attitude and adopt a conciliatory tone. For Emma's sake. And for the sake of proving to himself that he was a better man these days.

'I'm worried about Emma.' He came straight to the point as soon as they were inside. She hadn't invited him to sit, but that was fine. He had no intention of making himself comfortable.

'If that was true, you would have stayed away.'

'It's because I care that I came back.'

Moira harrumphed. 'You! You don't care about anyone but yourself.'

He ignored Moira's accusation — he'd discovered a long time ago that it was useless to try to argue with her.

'What happened to Emma after I left?'

Moira paled in front of him and sat down quickly, as though her legs could no longer support her.

'Nothing you need concern yourself with.'

Despite her visible distress, her words lost none of their bite.

He looked around the living room. Nothing had changed since he'd last been in here so long ago. The same furniture, the same photographs and paintings on the walls — it was as though time had stood still. Much as it had for Emma's personal life.

He turned his attention back to his reluctant hostess. She'd changed, though — even if her hostility towards him remained undimmed — her face was lined, her hair grey where it had once been blonde.

'Why didn't you tell me she was in hospital when I came back to see her?'

Her breath was exhaled in a long hiss. 'Because I didn't want you using it as an excuse to stay around.'

'Even if it meant I might have been able to help?'

Moira was on her feet again. 'She doesn't need your help, Nick Malone. If you'd left her alone in the first place things might have been different.'

He sighed. 'I'm not here for an argument, Moira,' he told her quietly. 'But neither am I sixteen years old any longer, and your power to intimidate me is long gone.'

Although, in truth, she'd never intimidated him. Even at sixteen he'd been well able to stand up to her — but all he'd ever wanted was for Emma to be happy. When Moira had told him Emma would be better off without him, he'd believed her.

Having seen the way Emma had lived her life since — the way she had refused to move on after he'd left — he now knew that to be nonsense.

'She doesn't want you, Nick — not really. Even though she says she does, she knows you're no good for her.'

'All I want is what's best for Emma.'

'Then leave her alone. Convince her there's no hope for the two of you and leave. She might be able to get on with her life then — meet someone else.'

'Why do you object so strongly to the idea of me and Emma being together?'

Moira's face contorted and her eyes closed briefly before reopening and pinning him to the spot. 'I don't like you. You're not good enough for her. She deserves much better.'

Nick knew when to cut his losses. He shrugged. 'Thankfully it's not you I'm trying to impress.’

As he watched, Moira deflated onto the sofa and he saw her for exactly what she was — a frightened middle-aged woman.

‘You’ve seen what she’s like. How weak she is. She’s not like other women her age. She won’t survive you breaking her heart a second time.’

‘Moira, I have no intention of breaking her heart. And I came back for her last time. Don’t you remember? You wouldn’t let me see her.’

‘That’s because it was entirely your fault that she . . . ’ Moira sat back and clamped her hand over her mouth.

‘It was my fault that she what?’ He had the feeling she had been about to reveal a part of the puzzle — the reason Emma had retreated and, apart from her work, insisted on living the life of a near recluse. But Moira had realised her mistake . . . and wasn’t saying anything else.

6

'I have no intention of hurting Emma again,' Nick insisted when her mother still didn't speak.

Moira didn't reply. She was looking decidedly grey, her breathing becoming increasingly wheezy.

'Inhaler.' The word was barely audible as she began to cough and clutch at her chest.

It was obvious she was suffering an asthma attack, probably brought on by the stress of having him subject her to an inquisition. Heck. He seemed destined to be in a state of permanent guilt around the Bradshaw females.

'Where's your inhaler, Moira?'

She waved towards the door and he stepped into the hall. Her handbag was on the stairs and he grabbed it and went back into the sitting room — taking the chance that she would be like all his other asthmatic patients who tended to carry their medication wherever they went. As she wheezed and coughed through the attack, he opened the bag, found what he was looking for and handed it to her.

The inhaler worked quickly and he was pleased to hear Moira's breathing returning to normal.

'How long have you been asthmatic?' he asked, once he was confident she was over the worst.

'Don't pretend you care.'

'I became a doctor because I care.'

Now he could see something he hadn't recognised when he'd been a teenager, and he felt sorry for her. She was scared of losing her daughter.

'She doesn't have to choose between us,' he told her quietly. 'We don't have to like each other, but we both love Emma and we can make her life easier if we try.'

Moira shook her head. 'Too much has happened.'

'We can put it behind us. For Emma's sake.'

She shook her head. 'No, we can't. Please, just go.'

Nick gave a brief nod. He might have his disagreements with the woman, but there was no doubting her devotion to her daughter. Nick couldn't hate her for that.

'Okay, Moira,' he told her as kindly as he could. 'But is there someone I can call for you?' He half expected her to demand Emma be sent for — it seemed in keeping that she would want her daughter to know and to worry. But she shook her head.

He gave her a long look. She seemed to have recovered sufficiently that he could leave without feeling guilty.

'Okay. You know where I am if you need me.'

She managed a bitter laugh. 'Ever heard the expression about it being a cold day in hell?'

It was only as he stepped back onto the street he realised he still didn't know why Emma had been in hospital. Had it really been his fault? Was that what Moira had been about to reveal before she fell ill? Emma had told him she hadn't deliberately harmed herself, but maybe she'd been so upset he'd gone that she'd been careless and had some sort of accident.

But would that explain why she was so determined to deny herself the happiness they could share? For the first time since he arrived back in Tullibaird, his resolve began to waver. Moira still thought he wasn't good enough for her daughter. Emma herself was adamant they couldn't be together.

Maybe the Bradshaw women had a point. He'd been sure most of his life that they belonged together, but what if he'd been wrong? What if the work he'd done to turn his life round hadn't been enough to earn her love and respect? Perhaps he should take a hint and accept that he and Emma had missed their chance.

Even as the thought tormented him,

he rejected it. He'd never accept it was too late. He'd spent too long living without her — he knew what a nightmare it was. Besides, he wasn't selfless enough to give up on his dream.

She was sitting in her car waiting for him when he arrived back home. Despite the unpleasantness of only a few moments ago, he couldn't help smiling when he saw her. She'd always had that effect on him. He reached for the handle and threw open the passenger door, an apology for keeping her waiting ready on his lips, but she spoke first.

'Kissing's now off the agenda.' Her tone was uncompromising.

Nick glanced across as he folded his frame into the passenger side of the Beetle. She was avoiding eye contact, retreating back into her shell. He wasn't surprised she was backtracking after last night's goodbye scene — she'd lost control and now she was running scared.

'I've always found 'hello' to be an

effective greeting.'

Her lips twitched. 'I don't want you to think I'm leading you on — or for you to want anything more than I'm prepared to give.'

He'd expected something like this. That was the only reason he'd stopped her ravishing him last night. If the evening had ended as they'd both wanted, her retreat may well have been absolute. This, they could recover from.

'I still think we should have gone on the bike.'

'And I still think we should be going in my car. I don't want to turn up at the hospital in black leather and helmet hair that looks like I've just tumbled out of bed.' He registered her little gasp of shock and saw the faint blush staining her cheeks and chuckled softly.

'Just a slight Freudian slip there, was it — eh, Em?'

She ignored the comment. 'Besides, I like driving.'

He sat back and shifted in his seat, trying to find a comfortable position.

'In that case, I'll learn to like being driven.'

She laughed. 'You'll never like being driven. You like being in control.'

'I'll make an exception for you.' His words ended with a gasp in response to the speed with which she took a sharp corner. She drove like a hell-cat, although her concentration was absolute and there was no doubt she was in control as she negotiated the narrow country roads. There was a lot about grown-up Emma he didn't know, and he looked forward to finding out. Probably best to let her concentrate for now, though.

Once they were out on the straighter main road, it was a different matter and the silence between them no longer seemed natural.

'I was surprised you climbed down that ravine.'

She shrugged a narrow shoulder. The thin straps of her blue top left much of her golden skin bare and he could see every hollow and bump of her collar bone. 'Had to be done.'

'You scrambled down that drop like a pro. I can't believe you could have done that, however urgent the need.'

'I joined a climbing club when I was a student. Managed to get to the top of the wall more than once.'

'Climbing club? That doesn't sound like you. What happened to the dancing classes?' She'd attended ballet and tap every Saturday as a child, he recalled — activities that, apart from the odd leap or high kick, kept both her feet firmly on the ground.

'Kept that up, too. In fact, I still do my ballet exercises.'

He could well believe that. She still moved with the easy grace of a dancer. But climbing club? That surprised him.

'You used to be scared of heights.'

The Emma he'd known had refused to climb trees, even when he'd urged her and promised he'd catch her if she fell. It had even taken him years to persuade her to join him at his favourite spot on the hill — and, even then, she'd refused to look down whenever they'd encountered a sheer drop.

'And then I found out there are much worse things to be frightened of than heights.'

'What things, Emma?' he questioned softly, hardly daring to breathe. 'What's worse than being scared of heights?'

She was quiet for a moment. He didn't speak. Was she going to spill? He'd known there was something — this was as close as she'd come to admitting he was right.

She made a sound that was somewhere between a sob and a sigh — and he wished she wasn't driving, so he could have taken her in his arms. She looked as though she could do with a cuddle. Although sometimes it was easier to talk if the mind was otherwise occupied. He hoped this might be the case.

'Not now, Nick.'

Ah well, obviously not. 'I'm trying to understand why you've changed.'

'We've both changed. We've grown up.'

He shook his head. 'It's more than that. You wanted marriage, babies . . . What happened to those dreams?'

He didn't flatter himself that she wouldn't have been able to fall for another man, if she'd had a mind to. Fourteen years was a long time, and a woman as stunning as Emma would not have been short of suitors.

They came to another straight in the road and she accelerated hard. 'Is that what you wanted? Did you want to come back to Tullibaird and find me with a husband and children? Would it have made you happy if I'd loved another man?'

It wasn't his imagination; her voice was filled with bitterness. He guessed she was still upset about Mel. Putting that to one side, he addressed her question.

'If you'd been happily married, I wouldn't have come back.'

Her sigh filled the close confines of the car. 'I might not be married, but I'm not free, Nick. I don't want a relationship — not with you or with anyone else. I'm fine as I am.'

Not exactly what he wanted to hear. 'But — '

'I don't want marriage and I don't want — ' She paused and sighed softly. 'And I definitely don't want babies.'

'Why not?'

'Maybe we can talk about it after we've seen Mary?'

He doubted her plan would work. Whatever she had to tell him, she wasn't finding it easy. And he had no reason to suppose it would be any easier for her later this evening than it was now — or than it had been at his place last night. He gave a brief nod just the same, but he needed to confess something.

'I went to see your mother before I met you tonight.'

She glanced across at him with a tense expression.

'Keep your eyes on the road,' he urged.

She did as he asked and diverted her

focus back to her driving, but he noticed her teeth sinking into her lip. Perhaps he shouldn't have confessed, but there were already too many secrets between them. Even if she was angry, her fury would be a million times worse if she found out from Moira. He had no expectation that Emma's mother would keep quiet — she'd likely relish the chance to cause trouble.

'Why?' she asked after a moment.

'I want to know what you're not telling me.' He prepared for fireworks; she would have every right to be unhappy. He'd gone behind her back; nobody would like that.

Yet Emma remained the picture of calm, except perhaps for a slight whitening of her knuckles where she gripped the steering wheel a little harder.

Then she nodded. 'Mum won't have told you anything.'

'She didn't,' he confirmed. 'But she had an asthma attack while I was there. I think it was my fault.'

Emma's glance snapped from the road to his face again. 'Is she okay?'

'Eyes on the road,' he reminded her. 'Yes, she was fine. Her inhaler worked as it should have.'

Emma was silent for a moment, concentrating on the road.

'It was probably more my fault,' she admitted at last. 'We had a row at lunchtime.'

Moira was doing a lot of falling-out with people. Nothing much had changed there in fourteen years, he thought wryly. He wondered whether she'd take advice on breathing exercises and relaxation techniques. He'd have a word with Angus, ask him to broach the subject, because it was highly unlikely that Emma's mother would take any kind of advice from Nick — not even if her life depended on it.

* * *

Mary was heavily sedated. They sat with her for a while. Against the background of the busy ward, Emma took her hand and spoke softly and reassuringly. She told Mary everything was going to be fine, that the part-time employees had rallied to keep the post office going, that Sadie was enjoying her holidays and being well looked-after . . .

When there was nothing more left to say, they got up to leave. 'Wouldn't it have made more sense to wait until she was awake and knew we were here?'

'I'll come again next week. I just wanted her, and everyone here, to know she was cared for. It's not nice to be in hospital so far from home, with nobody to visit you.'

'Is that what happened to you when you were in hospital? Were you alone and uncared-for?'

He winced, pained by the very idea and as he watched, her eyes darkened. Immediately he relented.

'I know, Em — not the time or the place.'

She gave a short nod of her blonde

head and he knew there was no point pressing the issue — not at the moment, anyway.

But she was going to have to talk to him — properly. And soon.

* * *

A wave of weariness enveloped Emma as she and Nick left the hospital. It had been an emotional few days and, despite her fondness for driving her car around the countryside, the prospect of the journey home was suddenly daunting.

'Do you fancy going for a drink?' she suggested to Nick as they drove out of the hospital car park.

'You're driving,' he reminded her and she cast him an exasperated look.

'Do you fancy going for a soft drink?'

They found a late night café — the kind that was all hard surfaces and harsh lighting that was not the most flattering. Nick, damn him, still looked utterly gorgeous, while she caught a glimpse of herself in the mirrored wall and saw that she looked like a washed-out dish rag. She averted her gaze.

They ordered at the counter — an orange juice for Emma and a double espresso for Nick — then sat at a secluded corner table.

'You won't sleep tonight.' She nodded disapprovingly at his cup. She didn't need caffeine to keep her awake — she'd barely slept for more than four hours in a night since Nick's return.

'Are you ever off-duty?'

She realised it must sound as though she was nagging him, which she supposed she was. She threw him what she hoped was a haughty look.

'Ignore me. I couldn't care less if you lie awake.'

He laughed softly and she gritted her teeth against the sound. She was going to have to let him go. The decision was made — it was the only fair thing to do. And then, when they had a bit of distance between them, she might be able to tell him about Nicholas.

He was drumming his fingers on the table. It was annoying; she wished he'd stop. But when he did at last, he leaned forward, as close as he could get with the table between them.

'I want you to come and meet my family this weekend.'

Her eyes snapped to his. What was he playing at now? This was completely out of the blue — he hadn't mentioned her meeting them before, and suddenly he was talking about this weekend.

Her tongue moistened her lower lip as she played for time. Despite her initial shock, meeting his family seemed like such a normal thing for her to do. The right thing. And yet, at the same time, it seemed absurd.

'Not a good idea,' she answered at last.

'It's a great idea,' he insisted, undaunted by her refusal.

Then she remembered, and seized on her excuse.

'Actually I'm busy this weekend.'

She'd been dreading the task ahead, but now it was providing her with a get-out for something with even more potential for upset. It was providing her with protection from the dangers of the unknown.

He raised an eyebrow. 'Genuinely busy? Or 'I don't want to meet your family' busy?'

She felt her face flush. It was true, if she hadn't been genuinely busy she would probably have tried to think up an excuse. But given her genuine excuse, she felt obliged to be outraged by his accusation.

'Genuinely busy,' she insisted. 'Staying with my friend, Jan, again. Remember? I did tell you.'

He nodded, and Emma gazed in complete fascination at the many dark blond tones of his hair as a lock fell across his forehead. She didn't want to think about how his hair felt beneath her fingers.

'Okay. I'm sorry I doubted you. You seem to spend a lot of time with Jan these days — you barely spoke to each other when we were at school.'

She shrugged. 'We moved in different circles back then.' She wondered if he remembered as she did that the two of them, Nick and she, had been pretty insular at school. Neither had needed anyone else. Looking back she realised that maybe it hadn't been healthy to be so engrossed in one person at that age. But looking at Nick, remembering the beautiful boy he'd been, she knew she'd be exactly the same if they had their school days to live over again.

'And you're in the same circles now?'

'We became friends after . . . ' She took a deep breath. 'After you left Tullibaird.' She swirled her orange juice around in her glass. 'She's married now, lives out in the country. I hadn't seen her for months until last weekend.' Her teeth bit into her lower lip as she wondered how much she could tell him before she broke down. She tasted blood.

'She's expecting a . . . Jan's expecting a baby soon. Her husband's going away for his brother's stag do. He's going to be away overnight and they asked if I'd keep Jan company.'

That had been the 'big ask' Jan had warned her of. It was only because she was so fond of Jan and Harry that she'd even considered agreeing.

'Next weekend, then?'

'Nick, it's not appropriate for me to meet your family. We don't have a relationship any more. We never will have. It's too late for us — we have to move on. Both of us.'

'Why?'

His eyes were so blue — she'd drowned in them before, but she struggled now against the attraction that threatened to pull her under for one last skinny dip.

She sighed and picked up her glass, just for something to do, swirling the liquid again, then put it back down without drinking any. 'What is it you've come back for, Nick?'

The look he sent her made her breath catch. 'You.'

'I kind of gathered that. But where do you see it going between us? What do you actually want? A quick fling? Or forever?'

Why was she asking him this? It didn't matter what he wanted — there could be nothing between them.

The girl came over from behind the counter. She smiled, seemingly oblivious to the tension between Emma and Nick. 'Can I get you anything else?' she asked brightly, looking from one to the other.

Nick shook his head. 'We're fine, thanks.'

'Actually, I wouldn't mind a coffee,' Emma decided. Nick raised an eyebrow and she shrugged. 'I'm not going to sleep tonight anyway.' *Thanks to you*, she added silently.

The girl smiled and promised to bring the drink over when it was ready. Emma waited until she was safely back behind the counter before daring to look across to Nick.

'Well?'

'I want the life we planned together.'

She sighed. 'Marriage? Children? Happy ever after?'

'Why not? Don't we deserve to be happy?'

'And the whole package is important to you?'

'Isn't it to you?'

She shook her head, unable to find the words.

'I only want to concentrate on my work these days. I don't have time for a family.'

He said nothing, only looked at her with those blue, blue eyes. She wished he wouldn't. It unnerved her — made her mindful of things she had no business thinking about.

'Thanks.' Emma smiled automatically as the girl brought her coffee over, but her expression sobered as she shook her head at Nick. 'I can't do it. I'm sorry.'

'What can't you do?'

'Any of it. It's not what I want.'

He leaned forward, his expression unreadable.

'Is it because of Mel?'

'No. Of course it isn't. It's got nothing to do with Mel — it's just the way I am now.' Distractedly she put two sugars she didn't want into her coffee and stirred.

'But it bothers you that I was married?'

She didn't like to know he'd been in love with another woman — made love with another woman . . . She flinched from that thought. But how could she blame him for trying to move on? His life as a small boy and young teenager had been torment. He'd been convinced by callous tongues and wicked gossip that he wasn't right for Emma . . .

No, however much she didn't like the fact he'd been married, she was grounded enough to understand these things happen when people have been apart with no hope of reconciliation. She couldn't hold it against him . . . but she didn't have to like it.

'I prefer not to think of you being

married to someone else,' she admitted at last. 'So I'm not going to.'

'We weren't together very long.'

Did that make a difference? Not really. He'd still been married — and she still didn't want to think about it.

'This is none of my business.'

'But I need you to understand, Em. We married the summer after we left school — and parted less than two months later.' He sat back in the uncomfortable plastic chair and knocked back his coffee in one. 'I wasn't a good husband.'

She laughed nervously, wondering what he meant. It was still none of her business, but now he'd made her curious.

'Why do you say that? Were you unfaithful or something?'

It was a question plucked out of thin air to fill the silence. She didn't imagine for a moment that he would have been unfaithful. When she'd known him — in those very telling childhood and teenage years — he'd been the most loyal and devoted of boys. Personalities didn't change to that extent and she had every confidence that the sinfully gorgeous man in front of her now shared the same traits of honesty and honour with the beautiful boy he'd been.

His eyes met hers — a clash of blue on blue. 'In a manner of speaking.' His steady gaze dared her to disapprove.

She didn't disappoint. Shocked, she gaped for a moment before recovering her wits. 'How can you be unfaithful 'in a manner of speaking'? You either were or you weren't.'

'It wasn't physical. I didn't sleep around.'

She stared across the table at him. 'So how were you unfaithful?'

'Because, every time I touched her, I closed my eyes and pretended she was you.'

His words hit at the core of her and the silence stretched as she absorbed this truth. Then she sighed softly.

'Oh, Nick. I really wish you hadn't told me that.'

'Why? Don't you want to know that you've lived in my dreams since I left you? That my body aches for yours . . . '

'Stop it, Nick. Please, stop it right now. This isn't helping.'

His blue eyes bored into hers, fierce and sincere, and she flinched from the truth they held. She didn't want his love — didn't deserve it. She hadn't been able to hold on to their baby, and she didn't deserve anything.

'Friends,' she offered when she could stand it no longer. 'That's all we can ever be. Just friends.'

He shook his head, his eyes not leaving her face. 'We'll always be more than friends, Em — and you know it.'

* * *

She was trying to ignore him. He knew she was. The care she took not to look at him drew attention to the fact. Every time he glanced her way, she was concentrating, scribbling furiously in her notebook with a frown on her lovely face. Despite it all, they sat in the practice meeting — a room's width apart — and the air between them sizzled.

If she didn't burn every time he touched her — if she didn't lose control after only a moment in his arms . . . perhaps he might be able to move on. Maybe he could even begin to believe that coming back had been a mistake.

But she did do those things — every single time they made physical contact. Her reaction had given him hope that, if he tried hard enough, he'd be able to win her around — whatever her reason for being intent on resisting him.

He glanced at Angus, who was discussing an incident that had occurred in the surgery — something to do with a patient who had arrived drunk for an appointment. Angus wanted a strategy in place to deal with any similar incidents that might happen in future. But Nick was only half listening. He was still shocked by Emma's insistence last night that they could be just friends. An absurd suggestion, when they couldn't keep their hands off each other.

He'd eventually agreed. If friendship was all she could offer him at the moment, then he would have to accept. For now. Friends first — and then they could see where it would lead to. His acceptance of her terms could only be temporary. Whatever she might say, they still loved each other too much to settle for half measures, and he wasn't about to give up on her. Not like last time . . . although he refused to imagine how their lives might be different if he'd persevered all those years ago.

He was still only listening to Angus with one ear, so when he heard his name mentioned, he gave a start. 'You seem to have settled in,' the senior partner commented.

Nick glanced across to where Emma was still finding her notebook to be the most interesting thing in the world.

'It's good to be back,' he said.

Angus smiled. 'And we're very happy to have you.'

There was a general murmur of agreement. Emma, he couldn't help noticing, remained silent.

'Tell me,' Angus continued. 'How are we doing with plans for the minor surgery clinic?'

'Everything's on track,' Nick confirmed. 'We even have a couple of patients lined up. One for a mole removal and another for aspiration of a ganglion.'

'It will be useful to have those sorts of things dealt with in-house again. We've had to refer more patients than we'd like since Sandy retired.' The senior partner looked around the room. 'Now, is there anything else anyone would like to discuss before we finish up here?'

When they all filed out of the room a few moments later, Nick watched helplessly as Emma dodged quickly away and he was left surrounded by the receptionists and Annie, the practice nurse.

'I'm having a few people round

tomorrow night,' Annie told him. 'It would be great if you could join us.'

He frowned at the three pairs of eager eyes looking up at him. He'd seen this before; a single doctor moved to town and suddenly he was fair game. Except he wasn't. Even if his ring finger was empty, in his heart he was definitely not available.

'Isn't Thursday a strange night to have a party?'

'It's not a party,' Annie told him. 'Not really. Just a few friends popping by for a drink to celebrate my birthday on Friday.'

'Then why aren't you having this get-together on Friday?'

'Emma's going out of town after work on Friday,' Annie reminded him. 'And I couldn't have people round without asking Emma.'

Of course, Emma was going to be there — that put a whole different slant on the evening. He grinned.

'Thank you for the invitation, Annie. I'll be there.'

But before he and Emma could enjoy themselves at Annie's party, there was tonight to get through. Whether she liked it or not, they had somewhere to go — and it was anyone's guess how Emma would react.

When last night he'd suggested meeting his family, it had been with a specific purpose. He understood her reason for declining this weekend. Even though it would have meant a longer journey, if she'd been amenable to seeing them the following weekend he might not have felt the need to press the issue. But she hadn't been willing — and this was important to him. Not least because he knew her mother.

Moira was the perfect example of a cold, controlling matriarch. Perhaps Emma's unbringing had lacked the alcohol abuse and the violence that had marred his own, but it had been equally dysfunctional in its own way. She had thirty years of Moira Bradshaw's influence to overcome.

But maybe, just maybe, if she saw

how normal and happy a family could be, she'd want that for herself. As she had done, all those years ago — before they'd been torn apart by circumstances. It was worth a try.

He popped his head around the door of her consulting room on the way to his own.

'Hey, Em.'

'What are you doing here?' she asked, frowning, her demeanour prickly as a hedgehog's. 'I've just called a patient.'

'Just wanted to let you know I'll pick you up from your place at seven tonight.'

The intensity of her frown increased, Nick noticed. She'd give herself a headache if she wasn't careful.

'Nick, I don't think that's — '

'Aren't we supposed to be friends?' he cut in, not allowing her the chance to finish her refusal.

'Well, yes. But — '

'I've only just arrived back in town. And I'm lonely. Coming out with me would be the friendly thing to do.'

She sighed; he could see her resolve to rebuff him weakening. 'Nick . . . I . . . well . . . '

He smiled and was pleased to see the corners of her mouth reluctantly curving upward in response. He took that as an agreement to his suggestion. 'And wear the leather,' he told her. 'Because tonight, I'm driving.'

With that, he dodged out of the way before she could object and smiled good morning as he met her patient in the corridor.

The man shuffled past, glaring daggers. 'Nick Malone,' he hissed as they drew level.

Obviously a fan. Nick resisted the urge to grin; he didn't think this patient would appreciate his perception of the humour in the situation.

'Dr Rudd,' he corrected automatically. He felt he should have known the man — they were around the same age, he judged, and there was something about him that was familiar — but when he tried to place him he drew a blank.

'Huh.' The patient, obviously not impressed, barged towards Emma's door with a huge scowl on his face. What a charmer.

He'd often faced patients who were grumpy and unwell, but this man had been positively hostile — and Nick was under the impression it had been personal. He shook his head as he went into his own room, making a mental note to keep an ear out in case the patient was overly aggressive during the consultation.

7

Emma reeled back in her chair as Greg Elder barged in — without the knock that usually preceded a patient's appearance. She did her best to mask her surprise with a bright and professional smile as she indicated the man should sit. He seemed agitated, however — even more so than normal — and he paced the floor instead, making Emma uneasy.

He always unsettled her, but today the feeling was intensified. Emma tried to shake the fear that something was very wrong, sure she was being fanciful.

'How are you today?'

'I see lover boy's back.'

Her eyes widened in shock at Greg's hostility. She hoped this behaviour did not herald a regression to his old ways. There had been a time he'd been a bit of a nuisance, but she had thought they were past all that.

'I beg your pardon?'

Greg snarled, showing a row of discoloured teeth. 'He took long enough about it.'

'Will you please sit down and tell me what the problem is?'

He stood still, but didn't sit.

'Nick Malone's my problem,' he spat with venom.

Never normally so slow on the uptake, the penny finally dropped for Emma. A few years ago, Greg Elder had taken a bit of fancy to her. She had worked very hard to get him to take no for an answer and had believed his interest had waned. It seemed she'd been mistaken.

'Okay. Well, if you'd like to sit, perhaps we can discuss the reason why you've visited the surgery today. I wasn't expecting to see you until next week. It's really too soon to know if those relaxation techniques have been effective in helping you sleep. You need to work on them a bit longer.'

'I don't want to sit. And the reason for my visit has nothing to do with your relaxation techniques. I'm here because of Nick Malone.'

Emma took a deep breath and forced herself to stay calm. 'What's your problem with Dr Rudd?'

'You're seeing him again, aren't you?' His eyes were hard and soulless.

She'd seen Greg in this state once before, but she hadn't been on her own with him in a consulting room that time. His chosen venue on that previous occasion had been the main street of Tullibaird, with people passing by within easy calling distance. Knowing help was only a cry away, she'd managed to talk her way out of it.

With another deep breath, she reminded herself she was not alone here, either. The building was full of staff and patients.

With care, she schooled her features into what she hoped was a model of neutrality and resisted the urge to get to her feet. Standing would allow her to use the body language of authority, but she was concerned any sudden movement might make matters worse.

'My relationship with Dr Rudd, or anyone else for that matter, is nothing to do with you. In fact, my personal life is nothing to do with any of my patients.'

She was proud of how calm and level her voice was, when all the while her insides were cringing with revulsion. She'd never done a single thing to encourage Greg Elder. When he had believed himself to be in love with Emma, she'd done her best to let him down gently. Eventually, he had seemed to accept there could never be anything between them.

Now, faced with the man ranting in her surgery, she realised she should have been firmer. However well he had seemed to take her rejection, she should have done more than have the receptionist encourage him to see another doctor — she should have refused to see him. If she had, he might not now be in a position where he believed he had rights over her private life.

'I'm afraid I have patients waiting. If you don't have a medical matter to discuss, then I'm going to have to ask you to leave.'

Greg Elder began to pace the room again.

'What is it about him? He couldn't even be bothered to stick around when you needed him. I would have looked after you, treated you like a queen. Offered you the world. Bought you anything you could ever want.'

Emma wondered how she should react to that statement. It was blatantly untrue that he would have been able to offer any of those things — Greg Elder had been largely unemployed for years and was in no position to offer anyone anything. It was a testament to exactly how disturbed he was that he was making these claims in all seriousness.

'He treated you like dirt — and you still act the tart for him as soon as he comes back.'

She realised she should be very scared.

'I beg your pardon?' she asked, playing for time.

His laugh grated on Emma's nerves. 'Look at you, all wide-eyed and angelic. But you have the soul of a whore. You led me on, let me believe there could be something between us.' His tone was menacing, no other word for it — Emma wanted to shrink back into her chair. 'And you lied.'

'No — I didn't,' she broke in, desperate to make him understand. She hadn't even accepted a date from Greg Elder — not least because the man gave her the creeps. 'I treated you with the same professional courtesy I afford all my patients. Nothing more. There never was and there never could be anything between you and me, Greg,' she told him. 'Quite apart from anything else, you're my patient.'

She cast a longing glance towards the phone. Dare she, while he was in this unbalanced state, risk making the situation worse by reaching out and making a quick call? She suspected she was going to need back-up in her dealings with Mr Elder.

She didn't get the chance — following her glance, his eyes gleamed with menace as he stepped closer and loomed over her. 'Don't even think about it.' He swiped the phone from her desk, ripping it from its socket in the process, and flung it hard against the wall. She watched as the receiver parted company with its cradle and it all landed in a sprawling heap on the carpet.

Well, she wasn't going to panic. Not yet, at least. She still had her shiny new mobile safely in the pocket of her jacket — and the button for calling patients on her desk, if it came to it. She still had a couple of options open if she really needed to call for help. And, of course, she could always scream — Nick was only next door.

In fact, she'd be surprised if he hadn't heard the phone being thrown against the wall.

She swallowed painfully. Greg Elder was still looming, his eyes flashing with anger, getting closer by the second. The stench of stale body odour made her feel sick.

'What is it about him?' She was revolted even further as drops of his saliva landed on her face. 'What's he got that I haven't?'

As she cringed even further into the back of her chair, Emma truly didn't know how to answer. She didn't want to be nasty about it — not even while he was holding her against her will — but this repulsive under-achiever and Nick were as far apart as it was possible for two human beings to be. She felt sorry for him. She was even frightened of him. But Greg was practically another species — he was self-obsessed to the point of delusion and believed the world owed him.

Whereas Nick was — well, he was just Nick . . .

There was a rap at the door and, as it

opened a fraction, Nick stuck his head around. 'Are you okay? Wondered what the noise was . . . '

Greg Elder moved fast. He was suddenly behind Emma, leaning over, one arm restraining her and pinning her to her chair. His other hand was at her throat and she could feel something cold and sharp against her skin.

Nick's intake of breath was audible and he stilled, the colour draining from his face as he took in the scene before him.

'Nobody makes a fool of me,' Greg hissed. 'One move from either of you and I'll slit her throat.'

Emma's pulse went into overdrive as adrenalin kicked in and she could feel pinpricks of perspiration on her upper lip.

Don't panic, she silently pleaded with herself, but a small sound of distress escaped her lips just the same.

The noise seemed to galvanise Nick into action. Carefully, almost in slow motion, he eased himself into the room, his shock replaced by blinding fury. Nick didn't lose his cool often, but when he did, the result tended towards the spectacular.

Now, though, he called on every scrap of self-control he possessed. Despite every instinct that urged him to tear in and rip the man's head off, he recognised the need for a veneer of calm.

The patient had a carving knife at Emma's throat. One flick of his wrist and she could be dead.

Nick briefly imagined a world that didn't contain Emma. Every protective instinct kicked in. She was not going to die today if he had anything to do with it.

He lifted his horrified gaze from the knife and made eye contact with the man. And suddenly he placed him. This was the man they'd seen shuffling past down the main street the night he'd walked Emma home from his place. Greg Elder, Emma had said his name was.

'Nobody wants to make a fool of you, Greg,' he said quietly. 'You need to put the knife down and then we can talk over whatever's bothering you.'

Greg Elder glanced down at Emma and then turned crazed eyes back towards him. For a moment, Nick wasn't sure the other man had understood — or even heard — not until he shook his unkempt head. 'No. There's no point talking.'

'If you tell me what the problem is, perhaps I can help.'

Greg's laugh was chilling. '*You're* the problem.'

Nick closed his eyes, just for a second, and he willed himself to keep strong. He took a deep breath, then he was ready to face Emma's captor again. 'Why am I the problem?'

'It's just so unfair. You've got it all, the looks, the medical qualification . . . and you have the girl. It's so easy for you.'

Nick raked his fingers through his hair. He could explain how hard he'd worked for his medical degree — how many hours he'd put in during his training. He could tell Greg Elder that if he, too, put in the effort, he might be able to improve his own lot. He could even admit that he still didn't have the girl. But there was no point arguing; Greg was in no mood to listen.

'If I'm the problem, then why isn't the knife at my throat?' Nick asked reasonably. Although he felt anything but reasonable. Blood was pounding against his eardrums, every sound magnified as he tried to think through his utter panic. Emma was in danger and, one wrong move from Nick could see her dead — his worst fear realised.

'Because she's the slut who led me on.'

'I thought I was the problem.'

'You are. Until you came back, we were getting along together very nicely. But you had to turn up and ruin everything.'

Emma's sound of protest was so tiny it would have been barely noticeable under normal circumstances, but it brought attention squarely back at her. She was so pale, startlingly so against Greg Elder's dark and rumpled clothing. Nick had to do something — and quick.

'So, if I was out of the way . . . '

He could see the other man's thoughts processing across his face. And he knew the exact moment Greg Elder reached the obvious conclusion. If Nick was out of the picture, the way to Emma would be clear for him . . .

'It's me you want to get rid of, Greg. Not Emma.' He took a step closer. 'Put the knife down. You don't want to hurt her.'

'Shut up.' Greg screwed up his features in frustration. 'I can't think.'

'It's me you want to hurt. Not Emma,' Nick reiterated. 'Let her go.'

Nick could see he was wavering. He lowered his knife a fraction, loosened his grip.

'I'm unarmed,' Nick pressed. 'I have no way to fight back. This is your chance to get rid of me.'

Greg Elder lunged towards Nick — and that was when Emma sprang into action. With breathtaking speed, she used her chair to swivel around and face the knifeman.

'No you don't,' she cried and from her chair, in one neat high kick, she knocked the knife clean from his hand.

In a reflex action Nick grabbed the other man in a stranglehold. Then he had him up against the wall, an arm locked at his back. He was a doctor because he wanted to heal people — it went against his every belief, but he so wanted to inflict pain on the other man. Pain and beyond.

If he was honest, Nick was tempted to punch Elder into unconsciousness and keep punching until he never woke up. With his instincts barely leashed, he glanced over his shoulder to find Emma shivering in her chair.

'Sweetheart, you okay?'

Emma nodded. He could see her lips trembling. He needed to take her in his arms and hold her close, but his arms were otherwise occupied. In frustration, he tightened his grip on Greg Elder and the man yowled in pain.

'Em — you need to call the police.'

* * *

Before they knew it, they had more help than they could handle.

'I hope he gets life,' Nick commented as they watched Elder being led away.

'I think he's ill, Nick,' Emma told him, still trembling. Her hair was starting to unravel from its neat bun and he'd never seen her look so vulnerable.

At last he was able to give into his urge. He gathered her up and hugged her close.

'I could have killed him,' he muttered, not quite steadily. The strength of his feelings shocked him. He'd always known he'd loved Emma, but now he knew he loved her more than life. He would have happily traded places with her earlier if it meant it kept her out of harm's way.

'He needs help, Nick. I should have picked up on it sooner, referred him for a physiological evaluation.'

'How could you know he'd do something like this?'

She pulled away, paced to the window. With her back to him, she started to talk.

'There was a time he followed me around, made a nuisance of himself. I should have realised he was volatile — I should have seen he was close to the edge. But it's been years — the girls on reception made sure he saw Sandy after that, and he's seemed okay since.'

'Em, you can't blame yourself for what happened today.'

She turned to look at him. 'I'm not . . . not really. I didn't lead him on, Nick. None of that was true. It was all in his head.'

'I know.' He hadn't suspected otherwise for a moment.

She pulled the clip out of her hair

and shook it loose before twisting it back and pinning it neatly where it should be.

'We should get on,' she mumbled, still visibly shaken. 'We're way behind with our appointments.'

'Tracey and Maxine have made new appointments for the non-urgent cases and Claire's ringing around for a locum. You shouldn't be working after everything you've been through today.'

Emma was still pale, but she smiled nonetheless. 'I'm fine,' she insisted.

He could see her hands were not quite steady.

'You don't look fine.'

'Honestly, I'll be okay. I'm better off working — it's the way I keep my mind off things.'

He nodded slowly. She was probably right. Best for her to get right back on that surgery horse.

'Maybe we should rethink tonight, though.'

Her nose wrinkled. 'In what way?'

'I'm offering you a get-out clause. I

know you were never that keen anyway. We don't have to go anywhere if you'd rather stay at home.'

She stepped towards him and her hands went to his lapel. With trembling fingers she brushed off imaginary specks of fluff from the charcoal cloth. When he'd appeared in her room, she'd almost been overwhelmed with relief; instinctively she'd trusted Nick to get them out of the situation. It was pathetic — he only needed to turn up and she just knew it would all be OK.

She leaned against him. 'You'll go out on your own instead?'

Even after all that had just happened, she just couldn't seem to keep away from him. It was shameful — any excuse to touch and caress him, even if she didn't get further than his clothes.

Emma needed his closeness. Greg Elder's behaviour had shaken her more than she cared to admit. Not only had Nick come charging through her door, oblivious to any danger he might be putting himself in, but he'd offered to take her place. It sounded dramatic even in her head . . . but it seemed he would have been prepared to die for her.

He shook his head. 'You shouldn't be on your own. We could stay in and I'll cook us something. You've had a traumatic experience — you need looking after.'

She sighed — if she was honest with herself, she'd like nothing more. But, while staying in and being cosy was all very well, she had to remember she was still trying to break up with him. Staying at home with him under these circumstances would be especially unwise when she was so impressed and grateful because he'd saved her life today.

It would be particularly dangerous when she already fancied the pants off the man.

She cleared her throat. 'You're going to stay with me this evening and be my protector?'

'If you'll let me.'

She bit her lower lip as she wondered if she should, perhaps, use her difficult day as an excuse to call off the evening after all. She could insist Nick go wherever he'd planned alone. But she had no intention of allowing a creep like Greg Elder to scare her into changing her plans. Even if she had been reluctant to go out with Nick tonight; even if she knew any sensible person in her position should seize the opportunity of a get-out.

She looked up into his blue, blue eyes. She could feel herself being pulled under.

'No — I'm fine, Nick.' She pushed herself away from him, stepped back. 'We should go out tonight. I'm not about to let Greg Elder's antics scare me into changing my plans.'

He nodded, then smiled. 'That's my girl.' He almost made it to the door before turning and their eyes locked.

'That was quite a kick. Elder didn't know what had hit him.'

'That's what twenty-seven years of

ballet exercises will do to a girl's legs.'

She smiled. The exercises had helped strengthen her muscles, of course they had, but Emma was well aware the reason her kick had been quite so strong was because a crazed knifeman had been aiming for Nick. And, just as his instinct had been to protect her, it seemed that her own instinct had been to protect him.

* * *

Despite her brave words assuring him she wanted to go out, Emma's resolve wavered again later. She really was trying to end things with Nick. She'd made her mind up — anything else just wasn't fair on either of them. So was it really wise to go out with him?

She'd assured him earlier that she hadn't led Greg Elder on, and she was still one hundred per cent sure she hadn't. But she was in grave danger of doing a ton of leading on with Nick.

She was sending out mixed signals

and even she didn't quite understand what she wanted. But she did know it would still be impossible for them to resume their love affair.

Accepting his invitation might very well give him the wrong idea. But on the other hand, he'd been right when he'd pointed out they were supposed to be friends. She'd be crazy to jeopardise her friendship with Nick — she needed that, at least. And, if he'd been any of her other friends asking for company because they were freshly returned to the area, she wouldn't have hesitated. Friends spent time together. They helped each other out.

She still wanted to be Nick's friend. That was why, at six thirty, she began getting ready for him to turn up to collect her. Although quite why she was so worried about her appearance when she was only going out for a platonic evening was a mystery. Her concern transcended her normal preparations of making sure she was merely presentable. She wanted to look nice for him.

Of course, there was no point doing anything much with her hair — not if they were going on the bike. But after she'd showered, she put on make-up and a generous spray of perfume. Then she poured herself into the black leather she still hadn't given him back.

She sucked her stomach in as she caught sight of her reflection in the mirrored wardrobe door. Lordy, but the outfit was unforgivingly tight, even on her slender frame. Well — there was nothing she could do about that.

She tried to tell herself the preparations she had undertaken were no more than she would have done if she was going out for an evening on a motorbike with anyone . . . except that she knew she was deceiving herself, because Nick wasn't just anyone.

Although she would have to make a conscious effort to try to treat him as though he was.

She didn't know how she was going to do that. Not only was he the man she had loved forever, but he was also the man who had been there for her today. Her hero. He'd shared those frightening moments when Greg Elder could have killed either one of them. An experience of that kind created a bond — whether she wanted it to or not.

Of course, he was also Nicholas's father. Even though he was still ignorant of that fact, they'd created a child together, and that had to be the most intimate act of togetherness imaginable.

The situation was impossible. Although she was way past wishing he'd never come back, spending time with him, when she knew she couldn't allow it to evolve into more, hurt so much. How was she supposed to pretend everything was okay?

Using the brush with rather more enthusiasm than was required, she tied her hair back into a low ponytail. All the while, she knew time was running out for her. Sooner, rather than later, he would discover exactly why Emma had become the talk of the town after he'd left.

Now, not only would he resent her for not having kept their son safe, he would also feel betrayed that she hadn't told him the truth the minute he'd arrived back in Tullibaird . . . but at least he would finally understand that she really couldn't give him the family he craved.

She should have told him sooner. Maybe not the minute he arrived back, but certainly when she realised they'd be working together, seeing each other every day.

With a shuddering breath, she tossed the hairbrush onto her dressing table. She would have to tell him soon. She couldn't keep putting it off.

Maybe she'd find the courage tonight, while they were out.

She could make it short and sharp — like ripping off a sticking plaster. That would be the easiest option for her.

However it would also be cruel in the extreme. She couldn't do that to him. She had to choose her words carefully;

rehearse and prepare how to tell him.

She felt nauseous at the thought — because, once she told him, it would be over between them. At the moment, he didn't quite believe that he wouldn't be able to fight through her defences. He still thought there was a chance for them. Once she told him, he'd know for certain that she meant it when she told him they had no future.

The doorbell rang and she opened the door. He stood, just as he had that afternoon in the surgery car park — tall and utterly scrumptious, broad, leather-clad shoulders filling out the doorway.

'Ready?' he asked with a grin that had her stomach flipping over.

No kissing, she was pleased to note — or any attempts at physical contact. Perhaps her insistence they could never again be lovers was starting to stick. Perhaps he was going to make this easy for her after all.

He maintained eye contact. She liked that. Most of the men she knew would have been leering, had she met them at the door dressed as a teenage boy's fantasy of a comic book super-heroine. But he didn't. He smiled — and his expression was a study in nice-and-friendly.

Unfortunately nice-and-friendly still made her want to swoon.

She nodded, but hesitated before stepping outside.

'Are you going to tell me where we're going?'

He ran his fingers through his too-long hair and her eyes followed the movement greedily. She remembered only too well how his hair felt beneath her own fingers. She forced her attention away and settled instead on his lips. Big mistake. His mouth proved an even bigger temptation.

'You're not going to like it,' he warned with a wry smile.

She frowned, more in response to the lustful direction of her thoughts than at him. 'Then why are we going?'

'My sister and her family have rented a holiday cottage not too far away.'

That shocked her mind away from any wicked temptations.

'Oh.'

'I know you said you weren't keen to be introduced to my family, but Lydia would really like to meet you. They're going home on Sunday morning so this is our only chance.'

He'd obviously given this a lot of thought — and taken into account that she was busy tomorrow night with Annie's party, and going to stay with Jan straight after work on Friday.

Her eyes narrowed. She was finding out all sorts of things about grown-up Nick — he'd never been manipulative when she'd known him before. She didn't know if she liked it. She hoped she didn't — it would be something to latch onto, an imperfection in the otherwise perfect Dr Nick Rudd. It really would be easier to walk away if grown-up Nick turned out to be a louse.

'It would've been nice if you'd asked me what I'd really like.'

'Sorry, Em.'

She hovered on the brink of stepping over the threshold. It would be so easy to go back inside — to slam the door in his face — but she didn't want to do that, not really. Whatever she'd said to him in the surgery, she didn't want to be alone tonight.

She decided to give him a chance at redemption.

'If I hadn't asked where we were going, would you have told me? Or were you just going to throw me in at the deep end?'

His face was serious, his eyes fixed on hers. Then, the corners of his beautiful mouth curved slightly upwards.

'I would have told you.'

Emma remained silent. Wanting to believe him, but not sure if she dared.

'I was planning to stop off at the beach on the way. The sea always used to put you in a good mood.'

He had to be telling the truth. She had no reason to suppose he had made that up. She smiled then; she couldn't help it. She'd always loved the beach — and he'd remembered, even after all this time. But was it a good idea to go and meet his sister tonight?

She looked down at the leathers she wore. 'I don't suppose you'd let me drive us in the car?'

He shook his head. 'It's the bike, or nothing.'

She shrugged. 'I'm wearing your sister's clothes, Nick,' she managed weakly, knowing most women would not be impressed to find their brother's companion so attired.

His lips twitched. 'She's worn those leathers once — ever. She probably won't even remember they're hers.'

He grinned, but his blue eyes gleamed with pure challenge. She knew he was wondering if she had the gumption.

The old Emma would have gone. The old Emma would have followed him until the end of the world . . . but she'd changed since then. The new, grown-up Emma was cautious. She had to be, because of everything she'd been through.

'So, Emma, tell me.' He leaned easily against the doorjamb. 'What is it you'd really like?'

Now she knew what he had in mind, she really wanted to stay at home — on her own if necessary. She wanted to keep herself safe and far away from the prospect of his sister's no doubt probing questions. If she had to meet his sister at some point in the future, she'd rather do it while wearing her own clothes. Yet this seemed to be really important to him . . . and, after this morning, she owed him.

Besides, if she was honest, she'd quite like to speak to a member of his family — to find out something of what he was like in those years he'd been away from her.

She exhaled through parted lips and looked up at him.

'I think I'd really like to meet your sister.'

Her reward was a grin that had

absolutely nothing to do with nice and friendly and she very nearly didn't make it to the bike on her very wobbly legs.

She mounted the bike behind him, and hesitated before putting her arms around him. She could just hold onto the grab rails, of course. But once they got going, she knew she'd be safer holding onto Nick.

It wouldn't be gratuitous hugging — not really . . . not if she needed to hold onto him for reasons of health and safety.

With a contented sigh, she slipped her arms around his waist, felt him warm and strong so close to her, and held on tight. She was ready for the ride of her life.

She knew the butterflies in her tummy had nothing at all to do with the bike or the prospect of meeting someone who was important to Nick, but everything to do with being close to him.

8

She was moulded to his back like a second skin and he only just resisted the urge to lean back into her embrace. He had to take this slowly — let her set the pace. He'd made the mistake of pushing her too far, too soon. It was a surprise that she'd agreed to go with him tonight, and he had to be content with that for now.

He'd warned Lydia that Emma might not be happy about the plan — especially as that creep Greg Elder had pushed them both to the limits this morning, dispatching thoughts of anything other than survival from their minds. Besides, Emma wasn't the carefree girl she'd once been. She was guarded and secretive — and she was very insular. Nick had been almost entirely sure that, once he told her where they were heading, she'd refuse.

Yet he'd had to ask. Even though she still maintained there was nothing between them any longer, Emma was a very important part of his life. She always would be.

He knew she was nervous; that much was obvious from the way her heart thumped an erratic beat against his back, even through the layers of protective clothing. If it wasn't for the loud roar of the bike he would have told her she had nothing to fear.

It was practically inevitable the two women would hit it off. Lydia was the most supportive of sisters and, even though she was five years younger than he, had saved his sanity when all he'd wanted to do was to curl up into a ball and die.

They leaned into a bend in the road and he made a conscious effort not to shudder as memories surfaced, uninvited, of the time immediately after he'd left Tullibaird, all those years ago.

It had taken him a while to come to terms with his mother's death — and the horror of the years he'd spent with her. After he'd recovered to a degree, he'd gone back for Emma — and been rebuffed and ridiculed by her mother.

It had taken weeks of visits and phone calls for him to accept she really wasn't at home. These days with instant messaging and mobile phones, it was easy for teenagers to keep in touch. Fourteen years ago, it hadn't been the case — at least, not for him. They hadn't even had a computer at home when he'd lived with his mother.

With each visit, each call, Emma's mother had turned every dark thought he'd ever had about himself back onto him. On Moira Bradshaw's poisonous tongue, the negativity had been magnified until he felt as worthless as he'd always been told.

When he'd given up, he'd truly believed the best thing for Emma would be to leave her in the peace her mother insisted she wanted.

Losing Emma had been harder to deal with than losing his mother. She'd been his world, his sanity, his salvation. To be convinced she didn't want him, that he was no good for her, had been devastating in the extreme.

He'd returned to the family home even more broken than when he'd first arrived. Convinced Emma was thriving without him, believing he would only hold her back, he'd been utterly bereft without her.

When he'd crawled back to his new family, it had been Lydia who had spent hours talking to him, reasoning with him, convincing him to go back to his studies. She'd barely been twelve years old at that point, but she had the intelligence and compassion of somebody twice her age. She'd refused to give up on him, even when he'd given up on himself.

He forced himself to put those dark memories from his mind. Instead, he took comfort from the roar of the bike's engine and Emma close behind him. They were his reality now. He didn't need to rake over the past.

The fact Lydia was staying in a cottage not an hour's drive away from Tullibaird was pure coincidence. It had been Lydia's husband who had booked the holiday as a surprise for his wife and their son. The odd thing was that he'd done so long before Nick had heard of the vacancy that would give him a passport back into the life of the woman whom he still, deep down, didn't really believe himself worthy of.

But Nick was no martyr, and he needed Emma. He'd spend the rest of his life striving to be worthy of her. Even if he hadn't quite managed it yet, he'd never give up trying.

He found Lydia's holiday cottage easily enough and roared to a stop in front of it. He sat for a moment, with Emma holding him so tightly it seemed she'd never let him go. But it was getting late and even though it was to be a flying visit, the sooner they went in, the more time Emma would have to become acquainted with Lydia, Jeff and Jack.

He pulled off his helmet and turned his head, just as she was taking hers off, too. Her face was so close he could feel her breath on his cheek.

'Ready to go in?' he asked.

'No,' she replied, but pulled away from him and got off the bike anyway.

He took her gloved hand in his — any excuse to touch her — and tugged her gently towards the front door. It opened as they made their approach; it seemed Lydia had been watching out for them.

She rushed down the steps to greet them and threw her arms around her brother in a giant hug.

'Hi, Lydia.' He laughed, fending off the attack. 'This is Emma.'

Lydia let go of him and stepped back to look at Emma. He could see the two women sizing each other up. Tentatively Emma held out her free hand.

Lydia took one look at the hand, shook her head, and then launched herself forward to embrace Emma in another enthusiastic hug.

Emma looked thoroughly startled, as well she might. Lydia was known for being tactile but Emma had obviously not been expecting such a friendly greeting from a woman she didn't know.

The first thing that struck Emma about Lydia was the physical likeness to her brother. There was no doubt at all that the two of them had jumped out of the same gene pool. The second was the hug, as Lydia threw her arms around Emma's shoulders. She stood, inert, wondering if she should perhaps hug back, but then Lydia pulled away and smiled into her eyes. Emma was left wondering exactly what Nick had said about her to his family to ensure such a warm welcome.

'It's so wonderful to meet you at last.' Lydia beamed. 'Come in — supper's nearly ready.'

Emma glanced across uncertainly at Nick, who offered a supportive grin. Suddenly she felt she could conquer the world. With her head a little higher, she followed Lydia towards the cottage.

Once over the threshold, she understood immediately why Nick was so keen on family life. Even though this was a rented, temporary holiday home, the warmth and security that enveloped her as she stepped inside was practically tangible. She could see why he would want this, particularly after the childhood he'd had.

It reinforced to Emma the very reasons why they shouldn't be together, however much he said it was what he wanted. Because, for Emma, this sort of family would never be an option.

'Emma?'

At the sound of Lydia's voice, Emma stopped chewing her lip and returned the other woman's smile.

'This is my husband, Jeff.'

Without warning, she was once again enveloped in a friendly hug. If her smile was a little stiff, it was only because she hadn't known family could be like this. Hers didn't hug; never had done. Even her lovely father hadn't been a huggy man — and her mother . . . Emma imagined that Moira's stiff back would snap in two if she found herself being spontaneously cuddled.

'So! We meet at last,' Jeff commented as he released her.

'I'm sorry?' Emma frowned.

'The girl Nick left behind,' Jeff explained. 'You've achieved legendary proportions in the family — but I was starting to think you didn't really exist.'

The rush of heat to her face provoked another laugh from Jeff. Emma wasn't accustomed to such teasing. Lydia dug playfully at his ribs with her elbow.

'Stop it. We're supposed to be showing Emma that we're normal and lovely. Not embarrassing her so much that she'll never want to see us again.'

Emma readjusted her expression into a polite smile. Then the shock of small, pudgy arms hugging her legs had her looking down . . . right down into the face of Nick in miniature.

She gasped. The intake of breath

actually hurt her chest. This was what Nicholas might have looked like as a toddler . . . the pain as she looked into that small, smiling face was unbearable.

She was struck again by how, since Nick had come back into her life, reminders seemed to be everywhere. Amplified and continuously goading her with the fact that she still faced the heartbreaking task of telling Nick.

She had no time to agonise, though. Nick scooped the little boy up onto his shoulder in an entirely natural display of affection. 'Hey squirt, I've missed you.'

The little boy giggled as Emma stared, shocked anew by the resemblance between Nick and his nephew.

'I'd like you to meet someone very special,' he told the child solemnly. 'Jack, this lovely lady is Emma.'

'Hello, Emma.' Jack leaned forward and held out a chubby hand. 'Pleased to meet you.' His little face so serious, Emma hesitated for only a fraction of a second before forcing herself not to react as her instinct urged.

She breathed hard, willed herself not to cry. Somehow, from somewhere, she managed to conjure up a smile for the child. 'Hello, Jack.' She took the small hand in hers and tried to forget she'd never held a hand this size before. 'And I'm very glad to meet you, too.' She shook Jack's hand with a seriousness matching that with which it had been offered.

* * *

It was later than they'd planned when they got back on the bike, but still, Emma didn't want to go back to Tullibaird just yet. 'You promised me a trip to the beach,' she whispered in Nick's ear as she slipped onto the bike behind him.

He half turned and she could see the curve of his full lips. But he didn't reply — instead he jammed his helmet on his head.

Right — so she wasn't getting her

visit to the beach. Probably just as well. There was a full moon, and moonlit walks along the sand would be asking for trouble.

With a sigh, she put on her own helmet, slipped her arms around him and held on tight, resigning herself to yet another journey where she was so aware of him that she wanted to peel her skin off to get closer.

He'd been right — Lydia hadn't noticed Emma had been wearing her leathers. Or, if she had, she'd been way too polite to mention it. However Emma's clothing worries had paled into insignificance compared with the emotional shock she'd faced at his sister's holiday home.

Jack had complicated her reactions — had been a living, breathing reminder of the little boy who should, by now, have grown into a teenager. Spending even a brief few hours with him had made her face the fact she had missed out on so much . . . and continued to miss out.

For the moment, she made a huge effort to put it all out of her mind. There would be plenty of time to think about her empty and childless future when she was alone in her cold bed. For now, she was going to wallow in being close to this man and she tightened her arms around him — just a fraction — sighing softly to herself.

This was as close to contented as she dared allow herself to be. For now, she wasn't going to think of the future.

She'd resigned herself to going straight home. So, when the bike veered off the road a short way out of town and skidded to a halt near a sandy cove, she wondered for a moment what was going on.

With one foot braced on the ground, Nick pulled his helmet off. 'Do you still want to visit the beach?' he asked over his shoulder.

It was impossible to see how blue his eyes were in the moonlight, but as they clashed with hers she felt a tugging low in her abdomen. A walk on the beach with him right now was such a bad idea. But, instead of urging him to drive on as she should have done, she removed her own helmet and grinned.

'You told Lydia you needed to get home.'

He smiled. 'I exaggerated. I love them dearly, but after the day we've had, I thought we needed to get away.'

She nodded, grateful for his thoughtfulness.

'So, Dr Bradshaw, do you want to go for that walk on the beach or not?'

She dismounted, pulled off her gloves, and held a hand out to him. 'Thought you'd never ask.'

They went down to the water's edge and allowed the sea to lap at their boots. It was dark, but the moonlight cast a silvery path across the water. Emma closed her eyes and listened to the sound of the waves for a moment.

'Was tonight a bit much?' Nick asked at last. 'I know my family can be a bit overwhelming.'

Emma smiled at the sound of his

voice. 'They're nice,' she said. 'I like them.'

She opened her eyes in time to see him nod. 'That's good. They like you.'

'Your nephew's just adorable.'

He moved so he was even closer, but still he didn't touch her. Even though it was too dark to see properly, she could see the glint of his eyes on her.

'You didn't seem to take to him.'

She drew in a sharp breath. She'd thought she'd done a good job of covering her shock and upset at seeing the little boy, but Nick had obviously realised something wasn't right. Her visible reaction to the child had been fleeting, she was sure of that, and she'd made an effort to speak with Jack. Yet Nick had noticed. It seemed that, even after all these years, he still knew her better than anyone else.

'That's not true,' she protested.

'Em, I saw your face,' he told her gently. 'When you first saw Jack.'

She was glad it was so dark, he'd be hard pressed to notice the flush warming her skin.

'I was . . . a bit taken aback to see how much he looks like you, that's all.'

'He looks like Lydia.'

'And Lydia also looks like you.'

He sighed. 'The family resemblance bothers you?'

'No,' she admitted. 'Of course it doesn't.' The reminder that Nick now belonged to a healthy family was something to be valued; there was no doubt about it. But how could she explain to him that Jack — a perfect miniature of his uncle — had reminded her vividly of exactly what she'd lost?

'But it does make me wonder . . . ' This was the right time to tell him. She could feel it in her bones. The opportunity she'd been waiting for ever since he turned up at the surgery. 'It makes me wonder whether our son would have looked like you.'

She heard his sharp intake of breath, but he remained completely still, didn't say a word. She wondered what to say next. In the end, she said nothing. He hadn't picked up on her hint — he'd thought she was speaking hypothetically. As they'd done so many times before he'd been torn away from her.

The moment was past. She wouldn't tell him tonight, after all. But soon. She would do it soon. Definitely.

She turned her head to gaze out towards the water — too overwhelmed by his presence to do anything else. He was just so big and so close — and just . . . *there*. It was impossible to think with him standing so close, looking at her with those frighteningly perceptive eyes.

Even though he still wasn't touching her, she could barely breathe. Would it really be so bad if she gave in to the need that had been thrumming through her ever since Nick had come back?

But even as the thought formed, she knew she should stamp over it with the highest of her size five heels. There was a very good reason why she'd shut herself away for years. And, even if Nick was back, even if she wanted to be with him more than anything, the very good reason still remained. She was no longer capable of giving him the love and the children he wanted — and deserved.

'Okay, Em. What if I said babies weren't a deal-breaker?'

She held her breath for a moment, the waves breaking on the beach the only sound marring the perfect silence. Then she turned back towards his large silhouette.

'What do you mean?'

'We don't have to have children. Lots of couples are happy living a child-free existence. We could be one of those couples.'

Sadness overwhelmed her and she shook her head. It was impossible.

'Nick, I saw you with Jack tonight. You're going to be a terrific dad — you're a natural with children. I can't ask you to give that up for me.'

* * *

He sighed softly into the darkness. She didn't want children and she wasn't going to change her mind — he accepted that now. He had no choice, after her reaction to Jack earlier.

In a way, he wished he hadn't seen her expression in that telling moment before she assumed her polite mask. But her reaction had been loud and clear for anyone who cared to notice and it had been stronger than just dislike of children. When Jack had hugged her legs, she'd been horrified — terrified, even.

Before tonight, he had thought perhaps they could talk things through, that maybe she'd have a change of heart. But there was no arguing with the kind of unguarded feeling she'd displayed back at the cottage. She didn't want children. He could see his dream of the perfect family fading. But he found the prospect of a family an empty one unless Emma was the mother of his children.

Even her wistful comment wondering

what any son of theirs might look like hadn't given him hope. If she'd made the remark yesterday, it might have been a different matter. But now he knew it had been an idle thought, nothing else. He'd seen the truth in her expression and the terror in her eyes as a pair of tiny arms had hugged her legs.

'You're not asking,' he told her. 'I'm offering. It's my choice to make.'

He wished it could be otherwise. But he'd found out a long time ago that you didn't get everything you wanted in life. And, if it came down to a straight choice, he'd choose her every time.

Her sigh reached him on the sea breeze.

'Nick, you've always said you wanted to be a father. Even as a teenager, whenever we talked about the future, you always said you couldn't wait for us to have our own family. How could you ever be really happy if I took that dream away from you?'

'I'd be happy if I had you.'

'Oh Nick, I can't be enough for you.

We've been through this.'

Her words pleaded for understanding. He wished he could make her understand that she would always be enough for him. Then he gave into the temptation that had plagued him all night and he reached out for her.

She fell into his arms as if she were a missing part of his own body, her face upturned ready to receive his kiss. But he didn't take her up on the invitation — not immediately. Instead, he pulled her pony-tail loose with one hand and wound her hair around his fingers, holding her fast.

'Why won't you tell me what happened, Em?'

He knew now beyond doubt it had been something life-changing. She'd proved today exactly how strong she was emotionally. She'd fended off an unbalanced patient, kicked the knife from his hand, and carried on with her working day as though the threat to her life had been the merest inconvenience. A woman who displayed such courage didn't crumple and give up on her dreams of a future without good reason.

She seemed to suck the breath from his lungs as she took a deep gulp of air and, despite having both feet firmly planted on the sand, he swayed, taking her with him. Her gasp had the effect of drawing his lips to hers with the precision of a heat-seeking missile, but rather than the thorough ravaging he ached to subject her mouth to, the kiss was sweet and restrained. Promising rather than demanding. Hinting at what might be, rather than explicitly demonstrating. He wanted her to know she could trust him, to know how much she meant to him and this was the only way he could think of to show her.

He wished she could find a way to talk to him, but he would be patient, wait for her to find the words in her own time. It killed him to know that she was hurting. Whatever she was finding impossible to tell him was eating at her, holding her firmly in the past. He wanted to take her pain away — free her, so they could move into the future together.

Her lips were warm and sweet, and he never wanted to let her go. He wanted to touch her, to feel her skin next to his. And he cursed the leather that, more than protecting her in the event of a collision, kept her safe from his touch.

When they were both breathless, he pulled away and rested his forehead against her head. 'We should go home, sweetheart. It's late.'

She nodded. 'In a minute.'

Then, with her arms still around his neck, she stood on tiptoe and kissed him with a thoroughness that drove him out of his mind.

How could she still insist they didn't belong together when she could kiss him like that? His entire body thrummed with need and still the kiss went on, her lips giving, her tongue plundering his mouth with a sweetness he'd almost forgotten.

More than anything, her kiss affirmed his belief he was right to fight for her. Whatever her words told him, her kiss sang a different tune. And that was the version he preferred to believe.

He didn't get up from the bike when he dropped her at her home. He didn't trust himself that far. She'd got him so wound up with her kisses and the way she'd clung to him on the bike that things would easily get out of hand. On past form, it was unlikely she'd call a halt — he'd been the voice of reason up until now, knowing she would hate him if he didn't respect her boundaries. Knowing it was up to him to stop things going too far until she was ready. But, if he got her inside the house right now, they wouldn't even make it as far as the bedroom.

'Will you be okay on your own tonight?' The quiver in his voice revealed a whole lot more than he would have liked.

'I'll be fine, Nick.'

'If you need me, call.'

She seemed about to say something, then changed her mind and smiled. 'Thank you, but I'm sure I'll be okay.'

'I've got a busy day tomorrow — we might not get the chance to talk.'

His surgery was booked out, as always — the locals seemed to have taken to him better than he could have expected. Or maybe they were just keen to get a look at the bad boy playing doctor. Whatever the reason, they called on him in droves. He and Emma would see each other, but only briefly and in the context of a busy GP practice.

She nodded.

'But I'll call round for you before the party and we can walk round to Annie's together.'

She shook her head. She was in retreat again and his heart dropped to his boots.

'What is it?'

'I've been thinking, I don't think it's a good idea for us to be seen arriving together.'

'Because of that Elder episode? We

can't hide away just in case it sets some loose cannon off.'

She shook her head. 'No — this has nothing to do with Greg Elder.'

If he didn't love her so much he might well have lost patience with her by now. Taken her at her word and moved on — as she claimed she wanted him to.

But he did love her . . . and it was things like her kiss on the beach tonight that had convinced him that moving on wasn't what she really wanted, either. Whatever she said, she'd been as sweet as honey in his arms.

'So, why isn't it a good idea for us to be seen together?'

She shuddered. 'Gossip.' The word was spat out — a world of bitterness behind it.

It was as though something was squeezing his heart — she was wound up so tightly that it actually hurt him to witness it. Nick had to stop himself from getting to his feet and hugging her close. Instead, he gave a short laugh, trying to make light of the situation. 'Em, I think we're both way past caring about gossip. Besides, I don't know where Annie lives.'

'You haven't had to put up with being talked about for the past fourteen years.'

'Em,' he told her softly. 'From what I've seen, the local people have a very real affection for you. If they have been talking about you, are you sure it's malicious?'

She hesitated. That had given her something to think about.

She gave a tiny shrug. 'Okay, Nick,' she agreed slowly. 'We can walk to Annie's house together. But only as friends — nothing more.'

'After that kiss on the beach?' She had to be kidding, surely?

'I'm sorry, Nick. When . . . when I tell you about what happened after you went away, I'm quite sure that us being anything other than friends won't be an option.' She lifted her head and walked to the door, unlocking it and walking inside without even turning her head to look at him.

So why didn't she just tell him what had happened? He swung his fist against his leg in frustration. It was crazy. She was so sure it would finish things once and for all — but she didn't know him. She couldn't begin to imagine the empty years he'd spent trying to find the courage to come back to her.

She obviously didn't understand the one thing he was sure of — that whatever Emma had done, whatever she'd been through, there was no way that being just friends was an option.

* * *

Emma didn't want to go to Annie's. She felt irritated at the thought of being around other people. In truth, she wanted Nick to herself — even though she knew now, more than she'd ever done, that it had to be over. The really irritating thing was that she knew that if she suggested staying at home, he'd take it as an offer and stay with her.

As he'd warned last night, she had only seen him in passing today. She should have been grateful for the peace and quiet. After all, her emotions had been all over the place since he'd come back — and seeing him had only made things worse. Yet she admitted — to herself at least — that she'd missed the warmth of their snatched moments during the working day.

He arrived on the dot of seven. She hated the way her heart fluttered in response to his smile.

'Hi, Nick.' She managed to muster up a smile of her own. However difficult she might find the situation, being friends was a good move. She had to keep telling herself that. The more she saw of him, the easier it would be for her to resist the slow grin that had her tummy flipping somersaults. It would be her own version of immunisation.

'You look nice,' he told her. His tone

was neutral — she was glad about that. No flirting or meaningful exchanges of glances. She could handle this. She could do platonic with Nick.

But then she looked at him — the strong shoulders, the breathtakingly beautiful face with its strong jaw and perfect cheekbones . . . Her resolve wavered.

'So do you.'

His arms were full of flowers and chocolates for Annie, and Emma left him on the doorstep as she went back inside briefly to pick up the wine she'd bought for her friend.

When she returned, she'd plastered a benign smile onto her face. If she looked the part of someone in the friend zone, eventually she might believe it herself.

'Which way?' he asked as they stepped through her gate and onto the street.

'Left. Annie's house is on the next street past your place.' They walked along in silence — although there was nothing awkward about it. Despite everything, she found Nick so easy just to be with. She always had.

He stopped as they approached the turning for Annie's street.

'I've wanted to ask all day . . . how are you feeling — after everything that happened at the surgery yesterday?'

She looked up and gave a little half-smile.

'I'm fine, Nick. What about you?'

'I wasn't the one with the knife held to my throat.'

She wanted to be flippant — to make light of what happened. But it wasn't funny and she shuddered.

'Let's just be grateful no blood was spilt. Yours or mine.'

Last night, she'd been so sure they would be able to do platonic. They'd nearly managed it — only that one slip on the beach. But they'd quickly recovered from that foolish interlude.

Her resolve to keep things platonic tonight had lasted even less time than last night — not even long enough to see her out of the door. Even so, she was proud of the way she'd ignored and overcome the powerful draw of Nick Rudd. She'd readjusted and moved the relationship back to platonic again.

But could she keep the barriers up at the party? She'd seen the way Annie and the other women at the surgery looked at him. The way they tried to get his attention and how they flirted. She couldn't blame them — he was gorgeous. And, after all, she was the one who'd insisted there was nothing between her and Nick so, as far as they were concerned, he was a free man.

Even so, she didn't like it. Even though she didn't feel able to want him for herself, she didn't like the thought of him with another woman — which was completely unreasonable.

In the space of five minutes, as they walked along the street in the evening sunshine, she made another complete U-turn. Platonic friendship wasn't enough. She wanted her mark of ownership all over him. The women at the party wouldn't leave him alone tonight, she was sure of it. And, however irrationally and unfairly, she wanted to warn them off.

9

'Here we are,' she told him as they reached a house half way along the terraced street. 'This is where Annie lives.' Although she was sure he didn't need her to tell him that — a heavy bass thudded through the walls and out onto the street, calling them to the gathering.

They were ushered inside and it was immediately apparent she'd been right in her assumption. Several pairs of female eyes turned towards him and it seemed he was suddenly surrounded by women.

They'd only just arrived, but Emma's jaw ached already from forcing a smile and she was exhausted from pretending she was going to enjoy herself. She hated herself for it as she looked around at the genuinely happy people dancing and chatting and drinking wine. These were her friends; people she worked with. Yet she wished them a million miles away.

Annie wandered into view, looking pretty in a loose, floaty dress. Emma forced her smile to be a little brighter.

'Hey, birthday girl.' She hugged Annie warmly, handed over the wine and stood back as Nick presented his own gifts.

'For you,' he told Annie as he handed over the flowers and chocolates he'd brought. 'Happy Birthday for tomorrow.'

The nurse lifted her face and Emma felt a stab of something suspiciously like jealousy as Nick brushed his lips in a lightning kiss against her cheek.

'What would you like to drink, Nick?' Annie was smiling up at him a little too brightly for Emma's liking and her hand had been on his arm just a little too long.

Uncharitably — and completely out of character — Emma felt like punching the grin off the other woman's face. Totally irrational. She hated herself for it.

Emma had always shied away from conflict unless it was completely necessary — as it had been in the Greg Elder situation. Faced with this additional threat to her relationship with Nick, however, she didn't feel particularly serene.

'I'd love an orange juice, thanks,' she told Annie a little too brightly, despite the fact she hadn't been asked.

She felt rather than saw Nick smiling down at her. Damn him. He knew; even without looking at him, she could sense he'd realised she didn't like Annie monopolising him.

'I'll have the same, thanks, Annie.'

'Okay, two orange juices it is.' Annie simpered in Nick's direction, barely glanced at Emma, and headed off to the kitchen.

She shouldn't be jealous. Annie was no man-eater; in all probability, she was only being friendly. But Emma was feeling particularly sensitive. Particularly as she knew she had no rights at all over Nick. If he and Annie wanted to ride off into the sunset together, it would be none of her business.

Hmmm . . . it was probably best not to think about that particular scenario.

He didn't leave her side. Despite the temptations, he didn't look twice at Annie or Claire or Tracey when they tried to attract his attention.

She thought she had to love him most of all for that. Even knowing she couldn't sleep with him — that she pushed him away at every turn — he was still breathtakingly loyal to her.

'So, look at you two, all cosy together after all these years.' Tracey wasn't one to hold her drink and her loud voice proved it. 'None of us expected that after everything.'

We're not together. The words formed on her lips, but she found she couldn't say them. She might try to tell herself there was nothing between her and Nick. She'd even managed to tell Annie the same thing. But she didn't want to deny him in public — particularly when any number of single females would be pleased to take her place. All the while, silently she willed Tracey to keep her mouth shut. Not to blurt out what was on the mind of everyone in the room — except for Nick. Not to elaborate about 'everything' that had happened.

Tracey beamed at the two of them before being carried off to dance by Annie's brother. Emma heaved a sigh of relief. She'd been given a reprieve this time, but she knew the situation had veered way too close to dangerous territory.

Her relief was complete when, only a short while after, Nick leaned towards her and spoke into her ear so he might be heard above the music and the chatter. 'Shall we make a move?'

She didn't need to be asked twice. The place was buzzing now and, even though she knew they might be missed, Nick's suggestion was too tempting to resist. Social situations such as this one were always guaranteed to have her on edge at the best of times. But with Nick sitting beside her, gorgeous and — as far as the others were concerned — available, her nerves were completely on edge. And, with the additional worry of who might say what on her mind, her head was just about ready to explode.

She sprang to her feet instantly and held out her hand to pull him to his feet. With a smile, he took her up on the offer of the hand, even though he didn't need her help.

'Let's go,' she said and forged a pathway through the dancing couples as she led him to the door.

'So that was Annie's idea of a few friends for drinks, was it?' he asked with a laugh as they made it out onto the street.

She let go of his hand and they began to walk towards home.

'Afraid so. We must be getting old,' she joked. Although if she were honest, she'd never been one for parties, even when she'd been Annie's age.

It was a warm night, but a sense of déjà vu made her shiver nonetheless.

Walking along the main street of Tullibaird with Nick, in the dusky half-light, pulled her back fourteen years. Same place, same people — it was almost as though nothing had changed. If she could forget the half-lifetime of heartbreak that stood between the people they'd been then and who they were now.

Yet it felt right to be walking at Nick's side. That was why she was finding it so hard to convince him they couldn't pick up where they'd left off, that they couldn't make a new start. In her heart she still felt they belonged together — even if, in her head, she knew that wasn't true. She shivered again.

'Cold?' Nick asked softly. She shook her head.

He shrugged off his jacket and draped it about her shoulders all the same. It was way too big and hung to her knees, but she didn't object because it smelled of him — of his soap and his cologne. It was still warm from his body

— his heat enveloped her like a giant hug and settled somewhere in the region of her tummy.

'You didn't enjoy tonight?' he asked as they walked.

She frowned. 'Was it obvious?' She might not have been the life and soul of the party, she might have grabbed the first opportunity to leave with both hands, but she'd have hated to think she'd been a noticeable misery.

'Not to anyone else. I think the others were too busy to give you much thought,' he reassured her. 'They were a bit . . . er . . . happy.'

She smiled, although she was unnerved that Nick, yet again, had picked up on a reaction she'd been convinced she had disguised.

'No doubt there'll be a few sore heads in the surgery tomorrow. I feel kind of guilty — Annie was going to have the party tomorrow, but changed it to tonight when she found out I wouldn't be able to go. And I didn't even want to be there.'

'No doubt she'll find a way to celebrate some more tomorrow night.'

Nick's pace slowed as they approached his home. She was surprised he wasn't going to insist on walking her home again, but she didn't say anything. Instead, she slipped his jacket from her shoulders and handed it to him. He hesitated, before reaching out, his hand deliberately brushing against hers. 'I don't suppose I can persuade you inside for a drink?'

'Can you keep your hands to yourself?' She smiled to soften the harshness of her words.

He frowned, made a show of pretending to think and she laughed.

'I can if you can,' he told her after a moment.

Of course she could. Piece of cake. As long as he didn't touch her, she was confident she would be able to resist his undeniable charms. Besides, the promise of another few minutes in his company far outweighed any internal battle she might be forced to wage.

Even as he unlocked the door, she

doubted the wisdom of her decision. She was already itching to run her hands through his hair.

Once inside, she accepted the glass he offered. She hadn't drunk any alcohol at Annie's party and she knew she could handle one glass without disgracing herself. Between sips of cool white wine, she realised he was watching her.

'What?' she demanded as she felt her face flame and a pulse kick into life deep in her abdomen. How did he do that? Elicit a physical response without even touching her?

For fourteen years, she'd successfully managed to forget that side of life. No man had ever come close to tempting. It scared her how easily Nick had managed to knock down her defences.

'Stay with me anyway.'

She couldn't have heard him right. She brought the glass to her lips and swallowed back a mouthful of wine too quickly. That was OK — choking gave her something to do that did not require thought. She spluttered to a recovery and his eyes were still on her, but he remained silent.

'What did you say?' Her face was red — it must be, from all the choking she'd been doing. Water streamed from her eyes. She knew she had to be at her most unattractive. Would he repeat his offer?

'I know you don't want to make love.' His gaze lingered on her lips and she swallowed again, only with no wine in her mouth this time, she was spared the luxury of another choking fit. 'We don't have to do anything you don't want,' he continued softly. 'But stay with me. We never got to spend a night together, did we? Just let me wake up, this once, with my arms around you.'

Maybe if he hadn't confided the other night just how miserable his childhood had been — or, perhaps, if he'd put pressure on her to change her mind — she might have been able to resist his suggestion. But, with her heart still aching for his lost childhood and in the face of his understanding about her celibacy — and her own yearning to be close to him — she didn't stand a chance. She wanted nothing more than to spend the night with Nick's arms around her.

He watched her intently, his gaze clinging lovingly to her face, and she felt his need echo through her own body. She needed to be near him every bit as much as he professed to need her.

'Yes.' The word lingered on her lips for only a moment and then he was at her side, drawing her to her feet, holding her so tight she could barely breathe.

She realised her mistake as soon as Nick undressed for bed — right down to his black cotton boxers. The sight of his teenage body hadn't prepared her for what he'd look like as a fully-grown man — and grown-up Nick with clothes on hadn't even come close to preparing her for the rush of need that surged through her now she could see every muscle, his toned skin, the hair that whorled over his chest . . .

The breath was sucked from her lungs and her lips parted in a silent 'Oh . . . '

'Em, stop it.'

Her lips were dry. She licked them. 'Stop what?'

He laughed softly. 'Ogling.'

She cleared her throat, unable to take her eyes off him. To her shame, she didn't even blush. 'I don't ogle.'

His slow grin made her toes curl. 'Come here.' He held out his hands and she walked over, kicking her shoes off before she stepped across the polished floor boards and into his arms. Her face was level with his chest. She rested her cheek on his bare skin and breathed in his masculine scent — wood tones and musk — as he enveloped her with his warmth.

'Are you sure about this, Nick?' She had to ask.

He brushed his lips against the top of her head. 'As I told you earlier, I can control myself if you can.'

She could control herself; of course she could. So what if her self-control had weakened like runny treacle the other night? So what if she might have ravished him on the spot if he hadn't put a stop to things? She understood her weakness now — which meant she would be able to keep it in check.

He released her and reached down to pull her dress over her head. A rush of cool air caressed her skin and she felt self-conscious as she stood before him in her bra and knickers. She was sure he must be able to see right through the lace, but she resisted the urge to cover herself and stood tall for his inspection. As she watched, his eyes darkened to the deepest blue and he took an unsteady breath as his gaze travelled over her body, clinging lovingly to every curve and dip.

'Ah, Em . . . '

She laughed. 'Now who's ogling.'

'I,' he took her hand, 'never ogle.' He grazed her fingers with his lips and led her across the room. 'Now, Dr Bradshaw, let's get to bed.'

The way he said the word 'bed' made her spine tingle. But they were just going to sleep, she reminded herself. Nothing else. She really believed that as they got under the covers and she cuddled in against him on the cool cotton sheet. She believed it as she felt his bare skin, hot and sinewy against her, and his forearm came around her, just beneath her breasts, and held her tightly to him. She still believed it even as he nuzzled against the nape of her neck.

Then she shifted against him and something snapped.

Heck, this was a terrible idea. Who was she trying to kid, thinking she could spend all night in his arms without throwing herself at him? Fourteen years was a long time to go without physical intimacy and she felt every minute of those years as she lay with him in his bed.

Yet the fear of falling pregnant still nagged at her.

Restlessly, she moved against him again and felt a thrill as he nudged back against her. A yearning gnawed deep in a place she'd forgotten could feel. She needed him. Now.

She was on the Pill; had been for years. Not as a safeguard against pregnancy, because she'd never intended to sleep with anyone again, but to regulate her menstrual cycle. The Pill was reliable . . . but, she knew, not a hundred per cent effective. Yet if they used a barrier method of contraception as well . . . She knew the odds of an accident occurring in the face of that double whammy was negligible.

'Em, keep still. You're driving me nuts, here.'

She turned to face him and lifted her hand to stroke his face. He'd left the lamp on, and she could see his pupils dilate as his gaze flitted to her mouth. Gently, she pressed her lips to his scar — wanting to make it better. Wanting to erase every bad thing that had happened to both of them. His breath was hot on her face. She couldn't stand it.

'Nick?'

'Mmmm?'

'Do you have a condom?'

Nick scrutinised her face with infinite care — watching out for any hint she might be joking. He couldn't understand the total turnaround in her attitude.

'Just how much did you have to drink tonight?'

He didn't think it was much, but maybe she'd sneaked something in the few moments he'd taken his eyes off her.

She laughed, the sound sending shivers down his spine. He'd always loved it when Emma laughed. It was something she didn't do enough of these days. 'A couple of glasses of fruit juice at the party and half a glass of wine downstairs.'

Exactly as he'd thought, but he'd had to make sure. However much he wanted her, he wasn't going to risk her pleading that she'd been under the influence if she regretted this in the morning.

She wriggled against him again, driving him slowly, utterly, out of his mind. 'I need you, Nick,' she whispered.

Faced with the woman he'd always loved lying in his arms, with her hair spread on his pillow, it would have taken a man with more self-control than he possessed to resist.

His hands trembled as he stroked the soft skin of her face.

'I love you, Em. I've always loved you.'

Her hands were in his hair, urging his mouth towards hers.

'I know. I love you, too.'

And that was his last coherent memory of the night — as he lost himself in the fantasy and the reality that was Emma Bradshaw.

* * *

Emma woke as light began to streak the morning sky. Nick was holding her tightly against him, as he had done all night. Fleetingly she wondered whether she could slip from his grasp and from beneath the covers without disturbing him. Retreat would allow her to avoid her most pressing problem — the inevitable talk about where they went from here. Nick had made it pretty clear he wanted more than friendship. She had made it equally clear that more wasn't an option. Things were bound to be difficult between them after last night.

The sensible thing would be to leave while he was still sleeping. Go home, have a shower, and get ready for work.

She wasn't feeling particularly sensible.

Instead she lay as still as she could, hardly daring to breathe. She watched his beautiful face in the dim morning light, until she couldn't stand it any longer and moved, only a fraction, to press her lips against his. He smiled in response and she realised she had never had the chance of a furtive escape.

'How long have you been awake?'

He opened one eye and his smile widened. 'A while. Why are you whispering?'

She laughed and experienced a delicious thrill of skin moving against skin as she did so. 'I don't know.'

He laughed with her. It felt so good that she never wanted to move from his arms . . . his bed. But real life was about to intrude; they were both expected at the surgery in a couple of hours.

'So, we love each other,' he said as the laughter died and they continued to drink each other in. He still couldn't quite believe she was here. He'd almost convinced himself she was a dream, that she'd disappear as soon as he opened his eyes. But his eyes were open and she was very much a reality.

'We do,' she confirmed. 'But saying it doesn't change anything.'

'It doesn't?'

He frowned and she pressed her lips to his creased forehead.

'We've always loved each other,' she reasoned. 'Haven't we?'

He drew in a sharp breath as her hand trailed over his stomach. 'We have. Definitely.' He shuddered at her touch.

'This doesn't mean everything's okay.' She rained tiny kisses along his jaw, pressed her lips to his scar and sighed. 'There are things I have to tell you. Things we need to discuss.'

'I know.'

It was important they take things slowly. Last night had changed the situation, but he knew there was still a long way to go. He nuzzled into her neck and felt her shiver.

'Oh, that's nice.' She sighed softly. 'Nick, I think you're going to hate me — once you know the truth.'

'Never, Em. Whatever you need to tell me, I could never hate you.'

That he was certain of. No truth could ever be as bad as living without her for fourteen years.

While she was driving him out of his

mind with her kisses, he went in for the kill and made sure she was incapable of anything other than moaning his name over and over.

* * *

She'd waited until the last possible moment before leaving him. She had just enough time for a shower and to get dressed in work clothes — and maybe, if she hurried, pack her bag because she was visiting Jan straight after evening surgery.

She definitely didn't have time to fight with her mother.

But Moira was lying in wait, right inside the front door — her face like fury.

'Tell me you didn't spend the night with him this time and I'll call you a liar,' she snarled as Emma shut the front door.

'I don't need this, Mum. I've got to get to work and I'm running late.'

'That's your own fault. I'm ashamed

of you, throwing yourself at him the minute he comes back. Why Nick Malone, of all people? You deserve more than a lowlife like him.'

At one time, her mother's words would have hurt. But no longer. Instead they made her so angry she could barely breathe. She just wanted Moira to leave. At the moment she didn't much care whether she ever came back.

'I'd like my key back, please.' She managed to keep her voice low and steady. No screeching or screaming, no ranting or raving. She managed to hide her fury and with her hand held out, palm upwards, she looked expectantly at her mother.

Moira's mouth gaped open. 'What?'

'My key. Nick's my friend — he's going to be a frequent visitor here. So, if you're going to talk about him like that then I don't want you letting yourself in here any more. In future if you want to visit, you can knock on the front door like everyone else.'

Moira's mouth gaped. She spluttered

a little, then at last found her voice.

'He's put you up to this.'

'Nick hasn't even mentioned you having my key. In fact, he's never criticised or bad-mouthed you in any way. Even though you deserved it.'

'How dare you speak to me like that?'

'I dare,' Emma told her, 'because you've asked for it.'

Moira shook her head. 'What have I ever done, apart from look out for you?'

'You sent him away, Mum. When I needed him.'

'He came to see me the other day. Did he tell you that, your precious Nick?'

Emma was pleased she was able to hold her head up high and answer truthfully. 'As a matter of fact he did.'

She saw Moira's eyes widen in surprise.

'Did he tell you he asked me about what happened?'

'Mum, you're not going to cause trouble between me and Nick so stop wasting your time. I love him, and I won't have you speaking about him the way you've been doing. Now, can I have my key, please? Then you need to leave, before you upset yourself even more.'

'I don't think I could be any more upset.'

Ah, the guilt trip. Emma had been expecting that.

'I'll ask Angus to pop over to see you later,' she said.

'No need, I'm fine.' Moira sniffed.

'Nick also told me about your asthma attack,' she added a little more gently. 'So I'm afraid I'm not giving you any choice in the matter. Now, will you please go so I can get ready for work?'

It felt good — even if Moira left the house seething with anger and Emma felt more than a tiny bit guilty for upsetting her. She'd finally done it — stood up to her mother and defended Nick. Even though she knew they had no future together, she still happened to believe he was worth it.

However she really wished she hadn't

needed to fall out with her mother again.

Morning surgery flew by with no complicated cases. Most of her patients were in to demand prescriptions for antibiotics to treat a virus doing the rounds. As lunchtime approached, she was fed up explaining exactly why antibiotics wouldn't work and why she couldn't comply with their requests.

Apart from the patients suffering the effects of viral infections, there was a young woman complaining of being tired all the time. Emma glanced at Lily Anderson's notes. 'You have three children under the age of five to care for,' Emma commented. 'I'd be surprised if you weren't tired. But we'll check you out to make sure everything's as it should be.'

She quickly examined the area under the patient's eyelids. 'You're a bit pale, so I'm going to take some blood to send away for tests.'

'What do you think it might be?'

'You may be a bit anaemic. It would

explain your symptoms. If I'm right, a course of iron tablets will sort you out.'

* * *

'I fell out with my mother again, this morning,' she told Nick when she met him at lunchtime.

He took her hand as they walked towards her house. 'Are you okay?'

She nodded. 'But I'm going to ask Angus to drop in on her later — just to make sure she is. After that asthma attack she had the other day — you know?'

It seemed like such a normal, couple-like thing to do — meeting at lunchtime, walking along the road hand in hand. But the very normality of it reiterated just how precarious a situation they'd found themselves in. They weren't a normal couple. And they were never likely to be.

She was living in a fantasy — nothing more.

Once he found out the truth about

Nicholas, she suspected he wouldn't be able to get away fast enough . . . and she wouldn't blame him one bit. It was so unfair that he was the last in town to know.

Even if he stayed, and continued to claim he was content to live without children, she'd always know the truth. Whatever he said, he wanted to be a dad — he wanted the family life he'd never had himself as he grew up. She couldn't deny him the chance to make that happen.

But, for this afternoon, she could make-believe she could have a happy and fulfilling life with the man she'd loved ever since he was a boy. She took him home and played house as well as she could, even if her talents in that direction were minimal.

'I'm embarrassed to offer you a sandwich after you made such a delicious meal for me the other night,' she told him as she handed him a plate. 'But I don't cook.'

'I can live with that.'

She sighed and she joined him at the table. He was so gorgeous — even though he'd missed the best part of a night's sleep, she'd still never seen anyone who came near him in looks or sheer charisma. He'd taken off his jacket, loosened his purple tie and undone the top button of his crisp white shirt. One darkly trousered leg was stretched out towards her, the other folded under his chair. And she longed to reach out to run her fingers over his thigh.

She sighed.

Even having only left his bed mere hours ago, she still wanted to rip the clothes from his body and to repeat last night's experience.

The harsh reality was, she would have to seriously consider sterilisation. It would be asking for trouble to continue to see him — even with double protection every time they made love — without making sure pregnancy wasn't even a remote possibility. And no contraceptive was a hundred per cent . . .

Then she remembered she still hadn't told him about Nicholas. Once she had, conception would no longer be a consideration. Because, whatever he said now, he would hate her.

Her fantasy of happiness burst in her face. She wasn't being fair to either of them, to carry on like this. She had to tell him about Nicholas.

'Nick?'

He looked expectantly at her over his sandwich as he bit into the wholemeal bread.

'I . . . '

She still couldn't. So she had to do the next best thing — she had to stop them both falling too deeply into this make-believe love affair. Because, the deeper they fell, the harder it would be to come to terms with when Nick found out the truth.

'Probably best you don't.'

She had tried to make the remark sound casual, but there was no way he could have missed the catch in her voice.

His brow furrowed. 'I'm sorry?'

'Probably best you don't try to live with my inadequacies in the kitchen.' She toyed with her uneaten sandwich. 'It's no good, Nick — we need to stop whatever's going on between us. For both our sakes.'

He let out his breath in a slow hiss. Much as he loved her, she was infuriating. Blowing hot and cold. Just when he thought they were moving forward, she was trying to tell him they needed to end it. Again. Whatever had spooked her after he'd left all those years ago had done a good job.

'Emma,' he told her, mustering infinite patience from somewhere. 'We don't need to worry about any of that now. Why don't we just enjoy being together, without trying to define anything? We can see how things go.'

'That's just it, Nick, things aren't going to go anywhere. We have to stop it now — this thing.' She waved her arm. 'Whatever it is. Anything else just isn't fair on you.'

'You think you're being fair on me now?'

'I'm trying to be.' She was driving him mad, fidgeting, tearing her sandwich to pieces.

'Aren't you going to eat that?' He nodded at her plate.

She looked up blankly. 'What?'

'Your lunch. Aren't you going to eat it?'

'For heaven's sake, Nick. I'm trying to have a serious conversation here. My sandwich is truly not significant.'

'Okay.' He sat back, his gaze fixing on her face. She looked pale and strained — but that was maybe not surprising as he knew she hadn't slept much last night. 'Tell me why you think it won't work and I'll tell you why you're wrong.'

She gave up all pretences of eating and pushed her lunch away. 'It's really complicated. I . . . will tell you, but I need more time than we have in a lunch break.'

He really didn't understand her. He

was so sure that whatever secret she was hiding would have no effect on the way he felt about her, and she was so sure it would.

'Em, we've always had something special. Neither of us is getting any younger. Do we really want to mess around and waste even more time when we could be together?'

'I — oh, Nick . . . ' She buried her face in her hands and he resisted the urge to walk around the table and take her in his arms. She was on the brink of telling him.

He waited for her to speak. When she didn't, he reached across and pulled her hands away from her face and took them in his own. She was cold, and he rubbed her fingers with his thumb.

'I meant what I said last night. Having children isn't so important to me that I'd insist on it if it meant losing you.'

She flinched from his words and he watched with a mixture of horror and fascination as the shutters came down over her lovely eyes.

'When I've managed to get through this weekend,' she promised. 'When I get back from Jan's and we've got time to speak properly, I'll tell you.'

'You're going to make me suffer for the next two days?'

'I'm not finding it easy.' She shrugged, her face still devoid of colour. 'I haven't been able to talk about it for a long time.'

Not since he'd let her down all those years ago. With that reminder, he knew he had to let her have the weekend. It had taken him the best part of a decade and a half to get his head together; it was hardly fair that he expected a similar transformation in her in less than a fortnight.

'But Nick,' she told him quietly through trembling lips. 'When I do tell you . . . then you'll understand why it has to be finished between us.'

10

Emma arrived at Jan's in time for tea. 'Has Harry already gone?' she asked as she brought her bag in from the car.

'He left a couple of hours ago. Which is great, because we can have a girly chat without him interrupting us with his nonsense.' Jan's smile was broad enough to confirm her comment about her husband was very much of the light-hearted variety.

Emma was ushered towards the stairs and they climbed to the spare bedroom, Jan moving with a heavily pregnant waddle. 'Here we are,' she said as she threw open the door. 'The management hopes you enjoy your stay.'

Emma smiled, as she was expected to do, and looked around the pretty room with its floral wallpaper. She tried not to notice Jan's bump — but, however hard she tried, it was impossible to miss. Even in a week it had grown quite considerably.

'How are you feeling?' she inquired.

'Fine,' Jan replied breezily enough, but Emma, with the perceptive eye of a doctor, noticed the weary lines around her friend's mouth, the worried glint in her eye.

'I'm going to unpack,' she said. 'Then I'll put the kettle on and you're going to tell me how you're *really* feeling.'

Not that she was looking forward to the conversation. Although she was a GP, she'd cleverly managed to avoid the bulk of the pregnant women who came into the surgery. But Jan was her friend — her very best friend in the world, apart from Nick. Emma would not be negligent in her duties as a friend, however difficult the circumstances were for her.

'I've had a bit of backache since this morning,' Jan admitted reluctantly. 'I didn't want to say anything earlier or Harry wouldn't have gone . . . and he had to go — it's his brother's stag weekend.'

'You should have said something sooner.'

Jan shook her head. 'How could I? In any case, he's only a couple of hours away — he can rush back if he needs to. But I'm sure everything will be fine.'

Emma wished she could be so sure. Jan looked as pregnant as it was possible for a woman to be. In her professional opinion, there was only one way to go from there.

'I don't like the look of those ankles.' Emma delved into her bag. 'I'm just going to quickly check your blood pressure.'

'I feel fine.' Jan squinted as Emma advanced with the cuff. 'But you're worried about pre-eclampsia?'

'Not worried.' Emma attached the cuff around Jan's upper arm. 'Just being cautious, that's all. Now, hush up and keep still, or we might get a false reading.'

Emma took Jan's blood pressure three times — just to make sure — and all the readings were thankfully normal. 'Okay, we'll just raise these legs, see if we can reduce the swelling a bit.' Emma lifted Jan's feet gently onto the sofa before perching in the chair opposite.

'So, tell me, how are things with your mother? Has she accepted that Nick's back for good?'

'Not even nearly.' She quickly filled Jan in on recent events.

'You asked for your key back? Oh ho ho, I'm sure that went down well.'

'I'm surprised you didn't hear the argument all the way out here.' Emma was making light of it, but she was still upset. 'It would help if she didn't keep living in the past.'

Jan didn't say anything, but Emma saw her raise an accusatory eyebrow.

'Not the same,' she insisted. 'Besides, Nick's no longer in the past — he's very much here.' She smiled to herself as she remembered their one perfect night. And then her smile faded as she recalled that was all it could ever be — one night.

'You still haven't told him, have you?'

She and Jan hadn't been close friends in those days, but like everyone else who had been in Tullibaird at the time, Jan knew about Nicholas.

'I couldn't, Jan. I just couldn't.'

'You have to. I know you find it very difficult to talk about, but it's not fair to either of you that Nick doesn't know.'

'I don't know how he'll react. I know it's selfish, but I'm not quite ready for it all to be over yet.'

Jan shrugged. 'You never know — once it's out in the open, he might see it as the rest of us do. That it wasn't anyone's fault. That you've spent the past thirteen and a half years hating yourself for a tragedy you weren't to blame for.'

Emma refused to cry. She sniffed loudly instead.

'And you never know,' Jan continued. 'You might get your happy-ever-after with the man you've loved practically your entire life.'

* * *

Nick was tired. He didn't want to see anyone. But the knocking was incessant and, concerned it might be something urgent, he dragged himself off the sofa and went to the door.

Moira. He really didn't need this tonight.

'Everything okay?' he asked. She was Emma's mother, after all, and he had offered her help should she need it. It would be uncharitable to slam the door in her face — as he was tempted to do.

She looked furtively around, as though worried who might be watching. 'Can I come in for a minute?'

He stepped to one side and she walked past him into the cottage. She didn't look happy, he couldn't help noticing.

'Would you like some tea?' he asked as she sat, straight-backed, on the chair nearest the window.

'Thank you, no. I heard about what happened at the surgery — with that Greg Elder.'

Briefly Nick wondered how she was

going to blame him for that particular episode, then he decided he didn't care whether she did. 'Yes, that was quite a morning.'

'Emma didn't tell me. I had to hear it from Dougal McDonald in the street just now.'

'She probably didn't want to worry you.'

Moira pursed her lips. 'It could be that — or it could be because she's not talking to me.'

Nick said nothing.

'I want to thank you.'

He must have misheard. 'I'm sorry?'

'Thank you,' she repeated. 'For being there for Emma when that awful man took her prisoner.'

He stared at her for a moment, stunned. This was the first non-hostile remark she'd ever made to him — ever. But it was also superfluous.

'I don't deserve your thanks for that.'

Her smile was tight-lipped. 'You saved my daughter's life. Of course you deserve thanks.'

'It was instinct — none of it was thought through. It could have easily gone wrong. Besides, Emma might well have handled it herself if I hadn't been there.'

Moira shuddered. 'But she didn't — and you were.'

'She saved me, too, you know. The guy was going to come at me with the knife — Emma kicked it out of his hand.'

Moira made a tiny sound of shock and covered her mouth.

'Emma's not the delicate, helpless little girl you seem to think she is. She's resourceful and she's capable. And she's much stronger than you give her credit for.'

Moira shook her head. 'You've got no idea what that girl's been through,' she rasped. 'I know she's stronger than she looks, otherwise she'd never have made it through those years after you left.'

'And didn't it take strength to ask you for her key back?' he asked softly.

Moira flinched. 'She told you?'

He nodded. He guessed that was why Moira was really here — that she'd finally realised if she didn't accept Nick, she'd lose her daughter completely. That was okay with him. Emma had been upset at lunchtime, when she'd told him about the argument. Moira making the first move towards peace would mean a lot to her — and all he cared about was Emma's happiness.

'You do her a disservice every time you imagine she can't cope with a situation.' He sat in the chair closest to his guest's and leaned forward. 'Let her grow up. Allow her to be the woman you must know she can be.'

Moira nodded as she bit on her lip and refused to shed the tears that were threatening to overflow.

* * *

The contractions were coming fast now, only minutes apart. Emma took a deep breath and willed herself to stay calm

— for Jan's sake if not for her own.

'The ambulance is on its way,' she told the mum-to-be. What she didn't say — but what Jan no doubt would realise — was it would take a while for it to arrive. Not only were they quite a distance from the hospital, with much of the journey down a winding, single track country lane, but the fog outside was getting thicker by the second.

This was the exact scenario she'd feared when Jan had asked her for this favour. That she would be left to cope on her own with a labouring woman — with full responsibility for the safety of both mother and baby firmly placed in her hands.

'I can't have the baby yet. It's too soon.' Jan's eyes were filled with fear.

Emma knew that had to be entirely her fault. Jan had to be remembering what had happened to Nicholas — just as Emma was herself.

It took her a couple of deep breaths before Emma managed to speak.

'It's a little early,' she confirmed. 'But

only a few weeks, and nothing to be overly worried about.' She was proud of how calm she sounded when really she wanted to run as fast and as far as she could from this entire situation. This was so *not* where she wanted to be.

'And Harry's not here.' Jan was becoming upset. 'I don't want him to miss this. I can't have my baby without Harry.'

'He's on his way back,' Emma reminded her friend. 'With a bit of luck both he and the paramedics will get here way before we need them.'

'It was my idea that he went this weekend,' her patient wailed. 'He didn't want to go, but I insisted. He'll never forgive me if he misses our baby being born.'

Emma bit her lip. She wasn't about to make any promises she couldn't keep, and it was in the hands of fate whether the expectant father would arrive for the main event.

Besides, if she was honest, she was more concerned about medical back-up arriving in time. She knew that, in theory, she should be able to cope with a straightforward delivery, and she hoped her medical training would kick in and override her personal issues — but she really couldn't rely on that happening. Not when those personal issues were so deeply ingrained.

She waited until Jan had ridden the crest of another contraction before she spoke again. 'I'm going to nip downstairs to get my bag. I'll only be a minute.'

Jan looked up from where she lay, already exhausted and covered in perspiration. 'You've got everything you'll need? I mean, if the paramedics don't get here in time?'

'I brought a maternity pack with me. No good doctor would visit a heavily pregnant woman without one of those.' Her attempt at humour was hollow — designed to reassure Jan. Emma was truly terrified — and she'd only ever been this terrified once before.

Despite having delivered babies as

part of her training, she had never flown solo where maternity issues were concerned. She'd always had support, and she didn't intend to set a precedent and take any risks now with Jan's baby.

With trembling fingers, she fished her mobile out of her jeans pocket as she raced down the stairs. There was only one person she could call — only one man who owned a Harley and who she could rely on to get here faster than the ambulance.

It only rang twice.

'What is it, Em?' Nick sounded tired — not surprising when it was two in the morning. She'd probably woken him.

'Nick — ' Her voice was a strangled sob. 'Nick, I need you.'

Nick was instantly awake. She'd used the same words as she had in his arms last night. But, although she'd said she needed him, it hadn't sounded like a romantic invitation this time. It sounded as if she was in trouble. Heart racing, he started to pull on his clothes. 'Where are you?'

She gave him the directions to her friend's house. 'Nick, she's having her baby now. I don't think the paramedics will get here in time. Please hurry. I can't do this on my own.'

Her panic was almost tangible. It didn't make sense. She was a confident and capable doctor, so why could he hear such fear in her voice? 'Are there complications?'

'No. The baby's a little early, but other than that . . . ' Her voice trailed off.

'I'll be there as soon as I can. But, if you need to, you can do this. You know that, don't you, Em?'

She made a sound — half way between a sob and a squawk.

'I'll leave the front door unlocked. Just come straight in — we'll be upstairs. Nick, hurry,' she pleaded. Then she was gone.

He powered up the bike and roared out onto the open road. A straightforward delivery with no complications. Why would a trusted GP be in such desperate need of help?

Yet she'd asked him to go to her — and that was a good enough reason for Nick to get there as quickly as he could.

Visibility wasn't good; a mixture of pitch-black sky and swirling mist was not conducive to safe travel. But he pushed the bike a little harder, riding as quickly as he dared.

He was nearly upon the remote cottage when he spotted a light burning though the mist. He skidded to a stop and pushed the front door open. The unmistakable sounds of a woman in labour met his ears and he took the stairs two at a time, following the sounds and knocking only briefly before going into the bedroom.

He'd arrived in time. It was obvious Jan was on the brink of giving birth — and Emma was standing by, pale and trembling and almost paralysed by what looked to him very much like terror.

Having made a lightning assessment

of the situation, he realised Jan's need was the greatest. He dashed to the bathroom to wash his hands and hurried back in.

'Where's the husband?' he asked Emma as he pulled on disposable gloves.

'On his way,' she replied through trembling lips.

He vaguely remembered Jan from school. She'd been in the year above. Whether she'd remember him, especially in her current condition, was debatable. 'Jan, I'm Nick Rudd, a doctor from Emma's practice. I need to examine you, is that okay?'

'I know who you are, Nick. We were at the same school.' Jan panted before turning to Emma. 'You weren't kidding — he's still utterly gorgeous. Aaaaargh . . . '

He waited for Jan to breathe through her latest contraction, before briefly looking up at Emma, but she wasn't taking any notice. He'd never seen anyone look so truly terrified before — her eyes huge in a face that was ghost-white.

'Em?' he called softly.

She turned her terrified gaze towards him.

'You OK?'

She nodded a brief response, but he could see she was a million miles from OK. Did her terror have anything to do with her assertion she didn't want children of her own? Had she assisted with a delivery that had gone horribly wrong?

'You don't have to stay in here,' he told her softly. 'Nobody's going to think any less of you if you want to leave the room.'

She took a deep breath. 'I'm fine.'

He was proud of her. So proud that, even though she was obviously petrified of something, she was working through her fear and wanted to be there to support her friend.

Time for him to take charge of the situation.

'It's not going to be long now,' he told them as he emerged from his examination of the patient. 'Em, hold

Jan's hand — she's going to need you.'

'I need Harry,' Jan wailed suddenly. 'He needs to be here. I can't have the baby until he gets back. I won't.' The tears streaming down her face were adding to Nick's feeling of total helplessness.

He sighed softly. 'I'm afraid it doesn't look as though you have much choice in the matter, Jan.'

Jan's eyes were suddenly furious. 'I refuse to have the baby now.'

'Your baby's ready to be born,' he told his patient quietly. 'And I'm going to need you to help.'

'No. It's not fair.' Jan's sob was heartfelt. 'I'm going to hold onto it until I'm ready. Until Harry gets home.'

'Jan, listen to me.' He spoke quietly, authoritatively — willing his own calm to transfer to his patient. Everything so far seemed pretty straightforward. But if Jan didn't start to co-operate, straightforward could change into something nasty — and quickly, too.

'Harry will want you and the baby to

be safe and healthy. You're going to need to push at the next contraction.'

'I can't. I don't want my baby to be born yet. It's too soon. And I want Harry to cut the cord, it's in my birth plan.'

'Birth plans are a good idea when it's a textbook delivery. But they often read like works of fiction when compared with reality. We have to make adjustments and do whatever's best for you and your baby.'

'But first babies aren't supposed to arrive this quickly. I've only been in labour for a couple of hours. Every baby book I've read says it takes much longer . . . '

'Unfortunately, your baby hasn't read those books,' Nick argued reasonably. 'Arrival etiquette kind of goes out of the window in situations like this.'

'This isn't how it's supposed to be . . . '

Nick glanced helplessly over at Emma. This wasn't good. Jan was becoming upset, and if she continued to refuse all efforts to get her to push, the result didn't bear thinking about. As he silently appealed to her, Emma gave a shake of her head and managed to push past whatever was bugging her. She took a breath that made her body shudder, then gave a tight-lipped smile. He noticed her hand was trembling as she reached out to push long strands of hair away from Jan's damp face.

'Listen, Jan. You have to do as Nick says. You need to push when he tells you.'

'But — Harry . . . '

'Harry's not going to blame you for giving birth to a . . . ' She took a deep gulp of air. ' . . . For giving birth to a healthy baby.'

A look he didn't understand passed between the two women. He was too busy at the business end of things to give it too much thought, but it unnerved him.

Whatever the look had signified, he was grateful when Jan began to co-operate at last.

'You're doing brilliantly,' he told her. 'Okay, that's the head out.' Jan pushed again and he delivered a miniature pair of shoulders. 'One more push should do it.'

He heard Emma gasp as a tiny body slithered into the world. 'A little girl,' he told them. 'And she looks just perfect. Congratulations, Mum.'

Even though he knew it was too soon for the infant to focus, a pair of tiny eyes scanned the room in mild surprise. Then the infant screwed her face up and gave a healthy newborn yowl.

He noticed Emma's cheeks were wet as she brought a clean towel to wrap the baby. With the cord duly clamped and cut, she held the baby close, seemingly mesmerised. His breath caught as he saw the look on her face — a yearning that reached into his heart and ripped it to shreds.

Despite her reaction to Jack the other night, he knew then that, for some reason, she was lying about not wanting children. A woman who looked at a newborn with an expression like this on her face was not a woman who'd decided to be child-free through choice.

She didn't move — didn't hand the newborn across to the mother as he'd expected. Instead, she continued to hold the tiny girl, gazing at her face in apparent wonder. Seemingly oblivious to the fact Jan was craning her neck to see the child.

'Em,' he said gently. 'I think Jan's waiting to meet her baby.'

Still Emma didn't move. Tears continued their silent path down her cheeks.

'It's okay,' Jan said softly. 'Let her have a minute with the baby.'

His eyes narrowed. Something was so wrong with this situation.

* * *

Emma hadn't dared allow herself this close to an infant since the day her own son had been born. Even at the births she'd attended as a medical student, she'd been clinical and detached while a midwife had taken the babies and handed them to the mothers as soon as they were delivered.

While returning to live and work in Tullibaird had laid her open to gossip and speculation, at least the other doctors at the practice had made her life as easy as possible. Angus and Sandy had known what she'd been through — and they had understood. So, between them, they'd dealt with the pregnant mothers and the newborns in the area and she'd been allowed to give those cases a wide berth.

She wasn't allowed the luxury of detachment now, not with Jan's baby . . . and, once she'd held the baby so close, she knew she'd never be able to count on her detachment ever again.

Emma had forgotten how tiny a newborn was, how warm and right in her arms. She hadn't realised, not until she'd lifted Jan's daughter, how much she'd ached to hold a baby again.

A yearning ripped at her, quickly

followed by a startling realisation. She wanted another baby.

Not that she was tempted to make a run for it with this baby. She was very much aware this infant wasn't hers. But this new life, snuffling quietly in her warmed towel, brought back vividly the feelings she'd experienced when Nicholas had been placed in her arms.

She'd suffered that trauma when she'd been so young, and she'd stubbornly refused to give up those childlike emotions. She'd never moved on — she had concentrated on the heartache.

Yet there had been joy, too. She'd been so happy when she'd found out she was having Nick's baby.

When the medical professionals had warned her Nicholas didn't have long to live, she'd refused to believe them. Nothing could ever come close to the euphoria of the short time she'd held her child. She'd experienced a surge of emotion so incredibly powerful that she believed her love alone would save her baby.

Then, when he'd died, there had been such despair. Such aching hopelessness.

Despite that, now she was holding this tiny human being, she knew she would do anything to experience the joy of her own child in her arms again. Not as a replacement for Nicholas — that would be impossible. She wanted, and would love, another baby for its own sake and in its own right. As Nicholas's sibling.

It shocked her how these brief moments, cuddling this tiny newborn in her arms, made her realise just how much she ached for another child of her own. The need was overwhelming. The urge to create someone who was a part of her . . . and a part of Nick.

Slowly, as she gazed at the baby's tiny face, she became aware of the silence in the room. She became aware of Nick's and Jan's eyes on her and she knew she couldn't hold onto this baby any longer. It was time to let this little one be with her mother.

With a soft sigh, she lifted the baby onto Jan's chest and watched, her heart cracking just a little more, as Jan gently kissed her baby's head. Exactly as she herself had done with Nicholas.

Now she'd handed the baby over, she was bereft. Her arms too empty and too cold. Aching too much with need.

She shivered and hugged herself, trying to recapture the warmth that had left her when she'd finally relinquished her hold of the child. Helplessly, her eyes were drawn to Nick — who was looking at her with concerned eyes.

She offered a weak smile and a tiny shrug in answer to his raised eyebrow. Trying to let him know she was fine.

Even though she wasn't.

'You okay, honey?' Jan asked and the spell that bonded her gaze to Nick's was lifted.

She nodded and wiped at her damp cheeks with the backs of her hand. 'She's beautiful, Jan. Really beautiful. You're very lucky.'

'I know I am.' Jan's smile held a

world of sympathy and sadness and Emma, unable to endure it a moment longer, let her gaze fall on the baby.

As she did, the door opened and Harry rushed in.

'Sorry it took so long to get back. I knew I shouldn't have gone at all — I had a feeling . . . ' He stopped uncertainly at the end of the bed and gazed across at his daughter. 'I'm too late.'

'Come and say hello to your daughter,' Jan invited, beaming, all the drama of only minutes ago forgotten.

As Emma had known, Harry wasn't in the least affronted that they hadn't waited for him. He beamed across at his wife, then, not taking his eyes from his daughter, he advanced towards the bed with a reverence that was breathtaking.

Emma didn't want to be in the room. She suspected she and Nick were intruding on a very private moment as the new family bonded, but with Jan still in need of medical attention there was little choice. Emma busied herself with tidying up while Nick saw to the patient.

When the paramedics arrived, Nick took charge again and spoke to Jan. 'Baby's healthy, but I'd like to transfer you both to hospital. You may need treatment for a retained placenta. It should have delivered by now.'

11

With Jan, Harry and the baby whisked away to hospital and everything tidied up, there was nowhere left to hide.

Nick and Emma sat in the kitchen of her friends' remote country cottage with reviving cups of tea — both so lost in their own thoughts that the beverages sat stone cold and undrunk on the table between them.

She wasn't going to tell him; he knew that — not without prompting, in any case. He wasn't really sure he wanted to know. Yet he still hoped — despite her assurances to the contrary, he still hoped there might be a chance for them. That meant they had to face whatever had happened to her — whatever had turned her into the desperately sad woman who sat before him now.

He picked up the mug and drank the cold tea. It was disgusting, but he finished every last drop and slammed his empty mug onto the scrubbed table top.

'We need to talk, Em.'

She looked across at him with weary blue eyes and nodded. He watched her pale blonde hair swing around her shoulders as she did so — and the urge to wind it around his hands, to press his lips against hers, was so strong that he had to grab it by the throat and force it out of his mind.

The physical wasn't an issue. He knew she found him physically attractive — he knew he could reduce her to a quivering mass of need and longing, just as she could do to him.

This was about something more. He needed her to trust him enough to share with him her innermost thoughts and worries. To tell him what it was that was so terrible, it was stopping her from grasping this second chance they had at a future together.

'I saw your face, Em.' His voice sounded strange, unlike him. She was so pale she looked as though she might pass out. But he had to press on; this had to be done now. Even though he was starting to be frightened of what he might learn.

'I saw your face when you were holding Jan's baby. You need to tell me what happened, sweetheart.'

She nodded again and he was glad that at least she agreed with him about that.

'When you left . . . Fourteen years ago, when you left, I was pregnant.'

Stupidly, he hadn't expected that. Suddenly it all made more sense — her reluctance to become involved with him again. Her fear of having children. Her mother's absolute hatred of him.

He hated himself. He'd left her to cope alone — a sixteen-year-old girl with an unplanned pregnancy, a very sick father and a hostile mother.

Then he felt something more than worry about Emma.

He felt suddenly sick.

She'd been pregnant fourteen years

ago — with his baby — and yet there was no evidence they had a child.

Whatever the reality, the scenario unfolding in his brain was unthinkable. He had to ask.

'Em. Did she force you to have a termination?'

Her face was deathly pale. He held his breath.

'Who? Mum?'

He nodded.

To his relief, she shook her head. 'No. She's done a lot of things, but she'd never have forced me do that.' She took a deep breath, steeling herself for something big.

He waited. Waited until she was ready to tell.

'I . . . we . . . had a little boy.'

Had. Past tense.

The room was closing in on him. He couldn't breathe — he felt suffocated. He wanted to reach across the table and take her hand, but apprehension had rendered him immobile.

He cleared his throat. The icy grip of

fear squeezed his heart.

'Where's my son now?'

She wished she'd never started this. She was so not ready. He was going to hate her. She knew.

Her sob was desperate. She looked across the table, silently appealing for understanding.

There was a reason she never spoke about Nicholas for all those years — it was because she couldn't. She just went to pieces. Even that day when she'd spoken about him with her mother, she had been goaded into it, anger fuelling her words.

She opened her mouth, still unsure of what she was going to say.

His eyes hardened. 'Where is he, Em? You have to tell me.'

The words came in a rush. 'In the ground — buried next to my father in the family plot.'

The quiet was unnerving — she could hear the ticking of the kitchen clock and not another sound. Nick sat stone still. He didn't seem to be breathing and even the muscle that always pulsed in his cheek when he was stressed was still.

His sudden sound of distress cut through her — not quite a cry nor a moan, but something in between. He reeled back in his chair then doubled over, as though he'd been punched.

She could have bitten off her tongue. How could she have done that to him? Told him in so cruel a fashion that their son had died? She'd had years to get used to it, and the pain still had the power to render her useless. She couldn't begin to understand what he must be going through, to find out practically simultaneously that he was a father and that his son was dead.

'Nick.' Her voice was barely a whisper. 'I'm sorry.' Her chair scraped back and she moved towards him, placing a tentative hand on his shoulder.

He reacted by springing to his feet and gathering her to him, wrapping himself around her and holding her so tightly she could barely breathe as unashamed tears ran down his face and sobs wracked through his body.

Emma cried with him. The strange comfort of sharing her grief with someone who understood — Nicholas's other parent — shook her.

It took a while, but eventually he spoke. 'What happened?'

'It wasn't an easy pregnancy. They kept me in hospital from twenty-two weeks. When I went into labour a while later, they couldn't stop it. Nicholas was just too small. They let me hold him and he died in my arms less than two hours after he was born.'

The pain was still so real that she just wanted to die. It never got any easier. Talking about it, verbalising what had gone on that dreadful day, made her acutely aware.

'Was your mother with you? Tell me you weren't alone.'

'She would have been, but Dad had been moved to a cancer specialist unit down south. She had to be with him.

But the midwives and doctors were very kind.'

Her father had been destined never to meet the grandson he'd so looked forward to welcoming — he and Nicholas had died within minutes of each other, in hospitals hundreds of miles apart.

Nick let his arms drop from her and paced the floor. '*Kind?* You should have been with someone who loved you. Instead, you had to rely on the kindness of paid professionals.'

He ran an unsteady hand through his too long hair.

'*I* should have been with you.'

She shook her head. 'It wouldn't have made any difference if you had been there.'

He seemed stunned by her words and she was horrified when she realised how they must have sounded. Before she could explain, he'd recovered sufficiently to grab his jacket and head through the door.

She stared after him for a long time.

At least now he knew why there was no going back.

But she'd have to find him. There was no way she could make him hate her less, but she knew he would be grieving. She could be there to talk to him — it was the least she could do.

* * *

Everyone was right, he realised. He was no good. If he'd been a decent human being he would have been there for Emma. To share the burden of grief, if nothing else. Instead, she'd had to shoulder it all on her own. No wonder she was so distrustful. No wonder that, in the fourteen years he'd been away, she'd remained on her own.

He raked an unsteady hand through his bedraggled hair and raised his eyes again to the gravestone that bore his tiny son's name. He'd come straight back to Tullibaird, to the cemetery — drawn there by some need that was too deep for him to completely understand.

It was raining, but he barely noticed the water soaking his hair and running down his face. Soon, he'd have to move . . . but not yet. He wanted to be close to the baby he hadn't even known about until a few short hours ago.

He had been ignorant of the child's existence, denied the chance to look forward to his son's birth and to grieve for his loss. Yet, since Emma had told him the truth, he missed his son more fiercely than he would have thought possible.

It had to be a million times worse for her. She'd carried the child inside her — his child. She'd held their baby in her arms as life had left him. All when she'd been little more than a child herself.

* * *

'Nick?'

Her voice broke through his dark thoughts and he turned his head to look for her. She stood a short distance away and it looked as if she'd been crying; her nose was red, her eyes swollen, although any tears would have mingled unnoticed with the rain running down her face.

He'd told her mother she was stronger than she looked. Now, knowing what she'd been through, he realised the full truth of those words.

'Hi, Em.' He tried to smile, but his face hurt too much. Everything hurt.

He shouldn't have left her there, alone at Jan's house, but he hadn't known how to stay with her, what to say or do. He'd been desperate, too, to put some space between himself and the place where he had, at last, found out about all that had happened.

'I went to your house . . . ' Her voice trailed off. It seemed she didn't know what to say, either.

He gave a brief nod towards the gravestone. 'You called him Nicholas. You named him after me.'

Her sigh was soft and she spread her hands out, as though appealing for understanding. 'I wanted him . . . I wanted him to have your name.'

He nodded. 'Thank you. I'm glad.'

She took a half step closer. 'Nick . . . Nick, I'm so sorry.'

He'd let her down so badly — and yet here she was, apologising to him.

'What do you have to be sorry about?'

'Because our baby died. For the way I told you . . . For saying it wouldn't have made a difference if you'd been there — what I meant was that nobody could have saved him. Not even you.'

'I know that's what you meant. But I should have been there to support you. Heck — you shouldn't have *been* in that situation. I should have protected you.'

They'd only had unprotected intercourse once — that last time before he'd had to leave. He'd done the responsible thing every other time; taken care of her. That final time, though, their need and hunger for each other had overridden everything.

'I was equally responsible.' She knelt next to him on the wet grass. 'I've never regretted making love with you,' she told him fiercely. 'And I've never regretted — not for a minute — that Nicholas was born. My only regret is that I didn't manage to keep him safe.'

She looked so vulnerable. He had no choice but to gather her close and bury his face in her hair.

'Sometimes, however much we wish otherwise, some things are destined not to be. It wasn't your fault.'

She nodded. 'I know that now.'

For years she'd blamed herself. Finally allowing herself to see with the perspective of an adult — and a doctor — she knew nothing could have been done to save her son. Knowing that didn't make her feel any better about losing her baby, but it did make her realise she needed to stop blaming herself.

She breathed in the scent of Nick, her face against his chest, and she felt the stirrings of hope. Holding Jan's baby had made her realise that, not only was she grieving for Nicholas, but also for all the other babies she and Nick might have had together if their future hadn't been stolen from them.

Maybe those babies could still be born . . . and maybe, just maybe, she and Nick would be lucky and those babies would live. Not that she would ever forget little Nicholas — her heart would always miss and long for him — but maybe she could still have a happy life with Nick, and with Nicholas's siblings.

'Do you hate me?' she asked, her voice muffled against his chest.

His lips brushed the top of her head. 'How could I ever hate you? All I've ever wanted is to be allowed to love you.'

'I love you, too, Nick.' She lifted her head so her lips brushed against his in the merest promise of a kiss.

'Even though I wasn't there to help you through the most difficult time of your life?'

'That wasn't your fault.' She smiled sadly up at him. 'You're here now. We can help each other through the rest of our lives.'

'Em, you do this,' he told her softly. 'Give me hope, then snatch it away. Don't do it again — not today, please.'

She shook her head. 'Not this time, my love. Not ever again. This time I want it all — I think we both deserve it all. We can never bring Nicholas back, but we can have each other.'

She looked at him, uncertainty gripping her heart as she looked up and found his reddened eyes guarded.

'That is, if you'll still have me?' she murmured.

His mouth softened. 'Of course I'll have you. How could you ever doubt it? I've loved you from the moment I knew what love was. Nothing's changed.'

She knew Nick had much to come to terms with. But she intended to be with him, to help him work through his grief — however long it took. Just as his return to Tullibaird had helped her.

She got to her feet and pulled at his hand. 'It's been a rough night and an even rougher morning. Come on — let's go to bed and sleep until Monday morning.'

She wanted to show him the photograph she had of their son. Then she wanted to fall asleep with Nick's arms around her — and she wanted his arms around her every night from now on.

Standing up, he slipped his arm around her shoulder and held her close as they made their way from the cemetery. At the gate, he stopped and turned and offered a last look towards their son's headstone.

'We would have been good parents,' he said softly, almost to himself. 'He would have been loved.'

'He *is* loved,' Emma corrected him, tightening her arm around his waist.

Nick nodded. 'And, if we're lucky, we'll have another chance to prove we can be good parents. One day — when we're both ready.'

Leaving his bike and her car parked at the cemetery gates, together they walked back to her house through the rain, exhausted mentally and physically. But through the heartache, there was a glimmer of light.

For the first time in nearly fourteen years, Dr Emma Bradshaw's heart held hope for the future.

Other titles in the
Linford Romance Library:

SINISTER ISLE OF LOVE

Phyllis Mallett

Jenny Carr is joining her brother on the Caribbean island of Taminga to start a new life. On her way, she meets Peter Blaine, a successful businessman on the island. He couldn't be more of a contrast to Craig Hannant, whose business is failing. His wife had died in mysterious circumstances, and Craig is now a difficult man to be around — but Jenny falls for Craig, despite all the signs that she is making the biggest mistake of her life . . .

CUPID'S BOW

Toni Anders

When romantic novelist Janey first meets Ashe Corby, she is not impressed. But frustratingly, the hero in the latest novel she is writing persists in resembling him! As Janey gets to know Ashe, she comes to admire and like him. But when she attempts to help Ashe's son Daniel to realise his dream of studying horticulture, Ashe is furious at what he sees as interference on Janey's part. Miserable without each other, will love win through for them?

MISTLETOE MEDICINE

Anna Ramsay

Ever since he wrecked her romance with Dickie Derby, Nurse Hannah Westcott has harboured a thorough dislike of Dr Jonathan Boyd-Harrington — but she never expected to see him again. To her horror, he turns up as Senior Registrar at the Royal Hanoverian Hospital, and there is no way she can avoid him — especially when he takes an interest in the hospital panto. Hannah has the star part, but it would seem she must play Nurse Beauty to Jonathan Boyd-Harrington's Dr Beast . . .

LEAP YEAR

Marilyn Fountain

Tired of the city rush, Erin Mallowson takes a twelve-month lease on Owl Cottage in Norfolk to run her own image consultancy business. Her ex-boss and commitment-phobic boyfriend Spencer thinks she's mad. Keen to embrace the village lifestyle, Erin doesn't expect it to include the enigmatic Brad Cavill, a former footballer with a troubled past. But even though work and love refuse to run smoothly, it turns out to be a leap year that Erin never wants to end . . .